Miracle

Lane

A Miracle Interrupted novel

Edie Ramer

Blue Walrus
Books

~o~

A miracle is prophesied in a small village...
And everyone secretly believes
it's meant for them.

~o~

OTHER BOOKS BY EDIE RAMER

Contemporary
MUST WORSHIP CATS (a Miracle Interrupted novella)
MIRACLE LANE (a Miracle Interrupted novel)
MIRACLE PIE (a Miracle Interrupted novel)
MO'S HEART (a Miracle Interrupted novel)
YOU'VE GOT MURDER co-written with Karin Tabke

Paranormal
CATTITUDE
DEAD PEOPLE
DEAD PEOPLE IN LOVE (short story)
DRAGON BLUES
THE SEVENTH DIMENSION (short story)

Science Fiction Romance
GALAXY GIRLS
MIXING IT UP (a Galaxy Girls novella)

Short Stories and Essays
The Fat Cat in ENTANGLED, A PARANORMAL
ANTHOLOGY
(all proceeds go to Breast Cancer Research Foundation)
The Kiss in EVERY WITCH WAY BUT WICKED
(all proceeds go to Kids Need to Read)
Killing the Rat Bastard Disease in AUTHOR MOMENTS
Fighting Back in AUTHOR MOMENTS II
(all proceeds of the Author Moments books go to Cancer
Research UK)

For updates, go to http://edieramer.com

MIRACLE LANE

Copyright © 2012 by Edie Ramer

Cover design by Laura Morrigan

Excerpt from *Miracle Pie* Copyright @ 2012 by Edie Ramer

This is a work of fiction. Names, characters, places, brands, media, and incidents are either the product of the author's imagination or are used fictitiously. Any resemblance to actual events, locales, or persons, living or dead, is entirely coincidental.

ISBN-10: 1939328039
ISBN-13: 978-1-939328-03-8

ONE

The thin man wearing the tan constable uniform at Nia Beaudine's front door was a liar.

People told Nia she'd been a liar in her old life. Those memories had been lost along with pieces of her skull and brain matter. Her new self couldn't understand why people lied. Truths were hard enough to remember.

Why would this man – *any* man – want to pretend he was a constable in this village of only 629? Most of them odd. A place she should fit right in.

This man…he didn't look odd, but she knew he must be very odd. Not dangerous, though. For one second she considered closing the door on him, but every instinct told her she could trust this man.

Instead, she said, "I think my cat is trying to talk to me."

Her words seemed to hang in the air like bubbles. She studied his face, waiting for his reaction. Ready for anything.

He studied her back. Just watching.

Yesterday Nia had learned the word *cryptic* while doing a crossword puzzle in an exercise to expand her word skills.

Her cat was cryptic. A cryptic, talking cat.

The man blinked. Not talkative like her cat. Perhaps even more cryptic. The silence stretched out between them. Nina heard the birds chatter and small rustles of leaves. Probably a squirrel or animal running across the wooded lawn of the house her mother's aunt had bequeathed to her.

"Why do you think that?" he finally said.

Nia's arms prickled. She was sensitive to sound – as if to compensate her for losing twenty-five years of memories – and his resonating baritone made her skin itch from the inside out.

"Because I understand what she's saying," she said.

He nodded, his expression serious.

Better than she'd expected when the words tumbled out of her mouth. Any other person would frown, a conviction of her insanity stamped on their disbelieving face, and step back, as if fearful that crazy was catching.

She always wanted to tell them it was catching only if someone was trying to run them over in a car.

And to make sure it worked, that someone would back up and run them over again.

But instead of giving her the *loco* look, this man stared at her steadily. His full lips closed and pressed into thinness, his eyes steady on her face. Mournful brown eyes that matched his nut-brown hair.

He made her think of a tree. Solid but not broad. One that would bend but not break. And his face... Like his body, his face was long and lean. Deep lines of pain scored each side of his mouth, though she guessed he wasn't more than thirty. He couldn't be much older. Not with his skin clinging tightly to his bones. His nose was blade-like, half a triangle. His jaw resolute. His eyebrows and hair thick.

He was a man's man, making up for his few words with an excess of testosterone.

Pheromones shot straight at her. She could smell them. They twirled around her like invisible dust motes, capturing and captivating her, putting a magical spell on her, bringing to life senses that had been sleeping since she woke up in the hospital bed, the world fuzzy, her mouth dry, and no thoughts in her mind.

But her mind hadn't been silent, not with a scream shrieking through it that no one could hear but her.

Later, she recognized the scream must have been her own voice. Even later, she realized that must have been the last sound she made as the car ran over her.

She shivered, the memories upsetting, but not as upsetting as the way he made her feel.

This was not the kind of help she'd hoped for when she'd called the constable's number.

Maybe this was the trouble her cat had been warning her about.

If only Bast had been more specific.

This cat and human communication was new to both of them. They'd been living together for only three weeks. She'd just started to understand Bast's yowls and meows and mrows and an entire orchestra of sounds yesterday. Like the first few pieces of a thousand-piece puzzle coming together.

Maybe they would get better with time.

She shifted her feet, the silence pressing down on her. Early on in her recovery, she discovered other people hated silence. The need to fill the wordless void compelled them to speak. To say things they later wished were unsaid. To say the truth.

Apparently he'd reached the same conclusion, since he kept his gaze on her, not moving a muscle. As if the loser would be whoever spoke first.

The silence was like a chewed piece of gum...growing longer and longer and longer...

"What's the prize?" she asked.

"Prize for what?"

"For talking last."

His lips stretched slowly then kicked up at the edges. "You talked first. You tell me what my prize should be."

She glanced down at his shoes. She'd amused him. Maybe there was a prize for making him smile.

Maybe there were no prizes in life.

"Something's crawling on your shoe."

He glanced down, not twitching. The most unmoving man she could remember. Since her memory went back only eighteen months, she supposed there might have been others.

"Caterpillar," he said. "A monarch."

She peered down at the yellow, black and white stripes on the fuzzy thing. "How do you know?"

"By the colors."

She nodded. That made sense. Every day she found out something new. "I'll look it up on my computer."

"When you called, you said someone was trying to kill you."

Her head came up. "I called the constable, but you're not him."

His stillness became different. More than just holding his breath. As if his blood stopped pulsing through his veins and his heart stopped beating and even his soul closed up, hiding itself.

Then a shudder shivered through him. Like a car that wouldn't start, coming to life. He blinked and his lips parted. "Jerry and I are twins. Identical. How did you know?"

She'd learned about twins. Her therapist had advised her to watch TV to learn about life. And she did learn. One twin could be evil. The other could be good. But by now she knew not everything on TV was true, and she guessed most twins were neither good nor evil, but just people trying to get through life without being killed and not wanting to kill anyone else. People like her.

"You aren't identical. You have deeper lines on your face."

He frowned, as if the thought displeased him. She looked him straight in the eye and didn't take it back. Pretending to be what she wasn't was too complicated. Life – with all its strange scents and flashing colors and loud sounds – was already too complex.

"You're thinner than he is," she said.

His frown didn't smooth. "Anything else?"

"Your voice is deeper."

"No one's said that before."

"My hearing is very sharp."

He looked at her oddly. A look she got often. One that said *what are you?*

If they asked her, she would tell them she was like a book with most of the pages blank, the words wiped off.

"My sense of smell is sharp, too." Smells could be awkward. And unpleasant. Except food. Most of the time, the smell of food cooking was wonderful. If there really were a heaven, she wanted it to smell like an Indian restaurant. Or Italian. Or pumpkin pie baking in an oven.

If it were heaven, the smells could alternate days. Every soul could walk around in its own cloud of scent.

This man's scent wasn't unpleasant. She wanted to lean in and give him a good sniff to identify the smell. To imprint it in her memory. But the thought of getting too close to him made her skin prickle again.

"Is that it?" he asked.

She scratched her head on the left side. The thinking hemisphere, Dr. Whitcomb called it, the reason her thoughts weren't quite normal. As she scratched, she avoided the area where her head indented.

"I think I should wait for your brother to come. He's the real constable."

"My brother's sick today."

His deep voice snapped her gaze back to his face. Though he still looked into her eyes, she could tell he was lying. Maybe because he was staring too hard, watching to see if she believed him.

"If this was a TV show," she said, "he would be with a woman."

The shadows in his eyes lifted and the skin around his eyes crinkled, while the corners of his lips curled up. She warmed inside, an unusual feeling. She tried to figure out what it was so she could explain it to Dr. Whitcomb.

Happy. That's what it was. An ice-cream-melting-on-her-tongue feeling. Only this melting happened inside her chest, warming her heart.

Maybe she wouldn't tell Dr. Whitcomb after all.

She'd tell Bast instead.

Bast didn't say, "Uh-huh, uh-huh," after every sentence, as if she were analyzing her words like they were math problems. Instead, she had a way of saying *mrrow*. Meaning: *That's interesting. Go on.*

"So you came instead," she said.

"You said someone was trying to kill you."

"I didn't actually say that. I said someone had tried to kill me in the past. And someone was on my property last night."

The crinkles around his eyes deepened, as did the creases on the sides of his face. "Did you see anyone?"

"Bast heard whoever it was first. And then I did."

"You didn't call last night. You called this morning."

"I heard them leave last night." She paused. This was when the way he looked at her would change. But she had to say it because it was the truth. "I only called this morning because Bast told me trouble was on the way." His expression didn't change, but Nia didn't allow herself to relax. There was more. "What if it was the person who tried to kill me?"

The sense of lightness coming from him turned suddenly dark. Though no clouds dimmed the sun above them, the air around Nia chilled as she looked at the hardness of his face, as if his outline from the chin up were carved on a sword hilt.

"I'll protect you," he said. "I'll make sure that doesn't happen."

Now Nia relaxed. For this second, she thought she wouldn't want to be the person he caught on her property. For this second, she was fiercely glad he seemed to be on her side.

TWO

Nia's staring eyes watched Rob as if he were a cat about to pounce and she were a mouse. Still. Silent. Watching. Ready to scurry for the nearest hole at his slightest move.

Not taking his gaze off her, he sat slowly on the flower-patterned couch with a curved back. The flowers were bright and happy, but he didn't see happiness in her past, present, or future. Nor in the witch's house, as it had been called long before she moved in. It still looked like an oversized cottage from a fairytale, built to lure children in.

The odd-shaped trees outside had been part of the fairytale-nightmare image from his childhood. They'd taken over the lawn, waving their crooked branches like arms ready to scoop up curious little boys.

The place used to stink of mold, too. Leaves piling up, probably. But in his youth it had seemed to be an evil scent – the witch's scent.

Miriam, who'd left the house to Nia, had looked haglike and old when Rob was a kid. He realized now a medical condition must've curved her spine so it resembled a crooked cane, but even adults had stayed away from the house.

Though the lawn had been cleaned up since Nia moved in, Rob shivered. Not because of the house. He'd been shivering for years and hiding it. Until that last tour in the desert. Until the hell that was Afghanistan. Until that last explosion.

Since then, it had gotten worse. In the air above him, darkness swirled, always there, ready to pounce and wrap around him so tightly it would steal his breath away. The blackness so close he could smell it.

It smelled like death.

It swirled lower now. Touching down on his back and shoulders. Just enough to let him feel the weight. To let him hear the echoes of screams and cries made by the injured and dying.

To see the staring eyes of T. J. and Morrisey.

The twisting emotion expanded inside him. Like live, hissing snakes unfurling in his belly, with fangs out, ready to—

"Are you sick?" she asked.

He blinked and through the haze of darkness, saw...her. Leaning toward him. Two horizontal lines creasing her forehead. Concern on her face.

It pulled him back from the hellhole of Afghanistan – straight into a different kind of hell in the middle of Wisconsin.

With a conscious effort, he pushed away the darkness and the smells of death and fear. He inhaled, air filling his chest.

He reminded himself he was here to help this woman.

"You didn't ask my name," he said.

She tilted her head. "I met your brother Jerry once. You must be Rob Ackerman. I heard people talk about you."

He imagined what they said. The poor Ackerman twin who had so much going for him but would never be normal again, who hid from life in his brother's house.

For once, the gossips got it right.

"I keep notes," Nia said. She sat with her spine as straight as her short, dark chocolate-colored hair, her hands on her lap, the left on top of the right. With her pixie face clear of makeup, she looked like a schoolgirl. Yet she was twenty-seven. And from the wisps of rumors he'd heard, she hadn't behaved like a schoolgirl before the injury that had put her in a coma for three months.

Injury, hell! Attempted murder. The murder failed, leaving her like a newborn, needing to learn how to eat, drink, read, and take care of herself.

An urge stirred inside him, like a sleeping bear waking, the urge to protect her from anyone trying to harm her.

Her earnest gaze fixed on him. Waiting for him to speak, as if it were his turn.

Another urge stirred. Since he'd been released from the VA hospital, he'd been painting. Sitting in the back yard of his brother's two-bedroom cottage on the edge of town, painting trees, snow, clouds, animals, flowers. And sometimes furiously painting abstract lines and splotches that lunged out from the dark corners of his mind.

Now, for the first time in the past eleven months, he wanted to paint a person. Not just any person. He wanted to paint *her*.

"What kind of notes?" he asked as he thought about the pigments he would use for her skin. Oils, of course. Though perhaps watercolors would catch the elusive color of her gray-green eyes better, like the sea on a misty morning.

"Notes of everything," she said. "Dr. Whitcomb told me to take notes."

"Do you do everything the doctor says?"

"I said that wrong. He doesn't *tell* me to do things. He suggests." Her hands raised and opened. A ballerina-like gesture that gave him another image, another pose in which to paint her. "He says I don't see the big picture. I just see little ones."

"Does writing it down help you see the big picture?"

"Not really." She slanted forward, as if about to confide something important, her lips parted to talk... And then she stopped, her expression puzzled.

"You remembered something?" he asked.

She gave a small shake of her head. "You smell good."

Nothing about her expression or body language was provocative, but his lower body sprang to life. Another urge stirring to life inside him.

No mystery there. He'd been with women since he checked out of Hotel Afghanistan. Except for booze and drugs, he'd do anything that helped get him through the nights...

But somehow it made the next day worse. He didn't know why. He sure as hell didn't confide in the V.A. counselors about his after-sex issues. He sure as hell wasn't taking notes.

And he sure as hell wasn't jumping in bed with someone who lived in Miracle, the place where gossip exploded faster than lit bombs.

And he *damn* sure as hell wasn't doing it with a woman who was more damaged than him.

She sat straight again. "Shouldn't I have said that?"

"It's okay. But it's not what you remembered, was it?"

"Of course not. I've never been close enough to you to smell you before." Her eyes narrowed. "At least, I don't think so."

He shook his head and suppressed a smile.

She nodded firmly. "We were talking about my notes

and Dr. Whitcomb. Sometimes I see little pictures but never big ones. Dr. Whitcomb says to keep taking notes and someday it will happen."

"What if Dr. Whitcomb is wrong?" he asked.

She tilted her head and frowned slightly, her face showing puzzlement.

Another image clicked in his mind. Another painting.

His hand itched for his sketchpad and a charcoal pencil. Or just a scrap of paper and a pen. Even a paper napkin would do.

He didn't *want* to draw her; he *needed* to draw her.

Pushing the need away, he clenched his hands on his thighs. "What if they're all small pictures?"

Her expression changed, her eyes widening, and she scooted back an inch on the couch.

She must have seen his tension. Felt it. Maybe with her super sense of smell, she sniffed it. *Eau d'anger.* He'd reeked a lot of that since Afghanistan. The smell had gained strength with each tour.

"Do you believe cats can talk to people?" she asked.

"Yes."

She started to smile—

"What I don't believe," Rob continued, "is that people understand what cats are saying."

"They don't!" Nia looked surprised that he mentioned it. "Not normal people. But I'm not normal."

"I can see that. What did he tell you?"

"*She*. Bast is female. Bast was an Egyptian goddess with a cat's head and a woman's body."

"Goddess of what?"

"First she was the goddess of the home. But in the end, she became a goddess of war."

"She told you that?"

"Of course not. Cats don't care about what happened

before them. Only people do."

He nodded. That was unarguable. It was just too fucking bad that people didn't learn from history.

If they did, there would be no more war. No more killing. No more bad guys. And best of all, there would be no need for men and women like him to protect their country against enemies.

"I learned about the goddess on History Channel," she said. "Then I looked it up on the Internet." She stood and glanced around. "Bast," she called, a fuzziness in her raised voice. "I need you."

She stepped toward the dining room then shifted toward the hall. She moved like a dancer, her movements graceful and oddly provocative. With her slender, small-breasted body drowned in loose navy pants and a blue-striped, short-sleeved T-shirt – both dotted with short hairs in shades of gray and white – she certainly wasn't dressed for seduction. About five inches shorter than him and too thin, she reminded him of a fey creature.

If he reached out to grab her, he had the odd suspicion he'd be left with a handful of fairy dust.

With a swift turn back, she caught him staring at her. She put her hands on her hips. "Seen enough?"

He laughed and was as surprised by his laughter as by her comment. There'd been some grit in it. Some sophistication. She wasn't a fairy creature, after all. If he touched her, she would be flesh and blood and bone...and woman.

Doubts crawled into his mind.

Was she really as childlike as she seemed?

Had she really forgotten everything?

"I've seen enough for now," he said aloud.

Meow.

Nia whipped around. He stood. Not looking forward

to this.

He didn't know about Jerry, but this was the first time he'd questioned a cat.

THREE

Bast strutted into the room, her head and tail held high, and allowed this new person to admire her grace and beauty. She stopped in front of Nia, who knelt down. Paying obeisance, Nia held out her hand and waited for Bast's *mrree* of agreement before rubbing her fingertips along the top of Bast's head. Bast leaned into her fingers, letting Nia know she was going in the right direction. Nia's fingers curved down, rubbing behind her ear in the perfect spot with the perfect pressure.

Bast purred and started her pleasure dance, her eyes squinting in the wonderfulness of the moment. But even dancing, she kept her gaze on the guest.

Someone had been in the yard last night. The intruder had attempted to be quiet, but twigs had snapped and stones had tumbled. Though the days were warming, the nights were still cold, the windows closed, so she hadn't gotten a whiff of whoever was out there.

But she knew two things.

Whoever it was had made too much noise to be a four-legged animal.

Whoever it was had been up to no good.

Humans announced themselves by ringing the doorbell. Or they called on the phone ahead of time. They did not sneak around...unless they wanted to pounce on the human like a cheetah going in for the kill.

Nia straightened from her crouch then perched on the couch and patted the seat next to her. Her signal for Bast to join her, should Bast choose.

The man remained standing. *"You first,"* Bast said.

He looked at her and scratched the furry curved line above his eyes that reminded her of a dog's eye socket bones. With his sad eyes and his long face, he even resembled Goldie, a dog Bast had lived with for a few days before she chose Nia as her human.

"She wants you to sit down first," Nia said.

The man raised his furry brows then sat down.

Bast jumped on the couch. Nia reached out and her fingers slid along the outer edge of Bast's teeth, allowing Bast to rub more of her scent on Nia. Her warning to other animals that Nia belonged to her and they needed to keep their paws off.

"This is the talking cat," the man said, not a question.

"You don't believe me," Nia said. No inflection in her voice, but Bast, with her sharp hearing that no human came close to equaling, caught the droop of disappointment.

Bast didn't share her disillusion. Except for Nia, Bast had no expectations of humans. Not for a long time. Though she was young and perfect, she'd lived in too many homes. Each time it had been the human's fault it didn't work out. After the fifth time, she'd decided to choose her own human.

Finding the perfect human hadn't been easy.

During her search, some bad things had happened. Very bad things. But she'd never given up, and in the end she and Nia had found each other.

Last night someone had tried to get into their house. If Bast hadn't woken Nia and warned her so she'd turned on every light in the place, whoever it was might have intruded.

She'd already saved Nia. They didn't need help now. Especially help from a man.

He doesn't understand what I say, Bast said to Nia.

"Rob doesn't believe in talking cats," Nia said.

Bast gazed at her. *No one believes but you. You're special.*

Nia nodded, but her lips twisted into sadness. Bast jumped on her lap and reached her jaw up to rub her head against Nia's chin. Marking her. Letting Nia know she loved her.

"Can your cat count?" he asked.

Nia gave Rob a haughty look that was almost as good as Bast's. "She's named after a goddess. Of course Bast can count."

"My dad had a dog named Einstein, and he was the dumbest creature I knew."

"Bast isn't a dog."

A long silence stretched while Nia petted Bast. Tension built in the room, coming from the man. It affected Nia. Bast felt it in the tautness of Nia's muscles. In the shortness of her breaths. Bast wished he would leave.

Men were trouble for women. Bast learned that in her second home, when the man who lived there had kicked her. He hadn't kicked the woman while Bast lived there, but Bast knew it could happen sometime.

She didn't understand why human females kept human males around after having a baby. The men had done the only thing women needed them for.

Nia didn't even need this man for protection. Not when she had Bast.

"If the cat can count," Rob said, "it's easy to prove whether I'm dense or you're imagining things."

Nia's hand stilled on the back of Bast's neck, her breaths quiet compared to his slow inhales and exhales.

Bast meowed. *Do it.*

Was Nia afraid he was right? That she was imagining Bast talking to her? Was that why Nia was hesitating?

The fur on Bast's back bristled and she meowed again, not taking her gaze from Nia's face. *Do it. Now.*

Nia looked at Rob. "What do you want to do?"

"Turn away from me, toward the hallway. I'll hold up fingers and Bast will tell you how many."

Nia tilted her head at Bast. "Will you do that?"

You don't need this man, do you?

Nia hesitated then answered...a breath too late. "No, I don't."

Bast butted her head against Nia's arm to let her know she understood. Bast smelled the musk coming from Nia. Another musk scent came from the man.

The scent of animals who wanted to breed.

It was too bad that humans didn't fix themselves the way they did cats and dogs. The way Bast had been taken care of.

After all, which species did more harm? Cats or humans?

But there it was. Some things Bast couldn't change. Instead of brooding over the injustice, she would find a way to use this human.

She mreowed at Nia. *Tell him I'll do it.*

FOUR

A new sensation lit up Nia, like tiny bubbles popping inside her. It took a second to recognize it: *fun*. That's what it was. This game was fun.

"Go ahead." Nia turned her back and looked at the curved entranceway to the hall. Light spilled in from the long windows in the front, warming the right side of her face. As if a fairy godmother touched her with a magic wand.

Mrow, mrow.

"Two." Nia's voice was low, her heart beating fast. To her sensitive ears, it sounded like large thumps of a bass drum.

What if she were wrong?

What if Bast didn't really talk?

What if her damaged mind was playing tricks on her?

Her hands shook, and she curled her fingers. This wasn't so fun anymore.

Why didn't he say anything?

Mrow, mrow, mrow, mrow, mrow, mrow, mrow, mrow.

"Eight!" The word shot out of her mouth, and she hoped she counted right. With her heart thundering so loudly, she wasn't sure if she heard every *mrow*.

"Can't she say the numbers?" he asked.

Nia turned. Anger flashed through her, and she didn't like it. She was used to observing, not *feeling*.

19

"She got the numbers right, didn't she?"

"This is about her talking."

A hiss came from Bast. Then a string of meows that sounded similar, but they all had different inflections and depths and sounds that made them distinct. Just like when people talked.

She says she doesn't like you."

"That hiss didn't need a translation."

"I don't think you want to believe."

"I don't want to believe a lot of things in life, but I believe them anyway."

She stood. "Then you're wasting my time." She held out her hands. As if they'd rehearsed this a thousand times before, Bast leapt into her arms.

Nia's heart still thundered, and she watched him, wary. For a reason she couldn't explain to herself, she had wanted badly for him to believe her about Bast.

Instead he'd come into this with disbelief, his mind made up beforehand. And he'd leave still disbelieving her.

"I should search your house."

"It's not necessary. If anyone entered my house, I would've heard them. And if for some reason I didn't, Bast would certainly have heard them and told me – whether you believe that or not."

A loud meow of agreement came from Bast.

Rob stared at Nia for a long moment, then dipped his head and started to turn.

She sucked in her breath. She felt as if a door that had been open was closing and a light shining in had turned off, leaving darkness.

Bast stretched upward and curved her paws over Nia's shoulder, her sleek body lengthened, her head raised. Nia's breath shuddered out. She looked sideways and saw Bast's ears perked. Listening.

Nia listened, too. Above the beating of her heart, she heard the crunch of gravel beneath tires.

"Someone's here," she said.

Rob immediately stopped, his muscles tensed, his smell changed. In that one instant, he became dangerous.

"It could be your brother," she said, her voice low. "Did you leave a note?"

His face was stolid, not showing anything. Like a metal mask. "It's not Jerry. Do you get many visitors?"

"Sam Guthrie visited a few times with his daughter Katie. She brought an apple pie. The real estate lady was here. And last week some children were in my yard. They called my home the witch's house. Isn't your car outside? Whoever it is will see your car and know you're here."

A car door opened in the front.

"I parked by the garage." He nodded at the side of the house, toward the back.

Bast hissed. Her claws dug through the cotton material of Nia's shirt, then she jumped off in a slow curve and landed on the floor gracefully. She darted to the door.

Nia followed Bast. "I'll get the door. You hide."

"I'll get the door." His voice was hard like his expression, the danger back.

She didn't care. Something in her was taking over. Something she didn't know she had. "You're not the real constable," she said, making her voice low.

"You're not one, either."

"But I am the owner of this house." She didn't know where all of this was coming from, but it made her feel...alive. As if she were participating in her life instead of sitting back and watching. Taking down mental instructions of what to do, what to say, and what her face should express when it was her turn to act.

And just as important, what not to do, what not to say, and what her face shouldn't express.

It was all so confusing. Too confusing to try. But Dr. Whitcomb had been telling her she needed to get off the sidelines and start dancing.

She was hopping onto the dance floor now. Ready to cha-cha-cha, tango, and if necessary, do a few high kicks.

"I was a sergeant in the US Army," he said. "If anyone came here to hurt you, I know how to deal with it."

The doorbell rang. He stepped forward, and she grabbed his upper arm, feeling the hardness of his bicep beneath the thick cotton sleeve.

"It could be the mail lady. Are you going to deal with her?"

He looked her full in the face. He inhaled, his nostrils flaring. When he exhaled, some of his tension eased. "The mail lady is my cousin's wife." His voice turned calmer. Under her fingers, the knotted bicep eased. "She has two kids, and if I said one wrong word to her, it would ruin my mother's Fourth of July picnic."

"Is everyone in this town connected by marriage?" Laughter built inside her. Hysterical laughter. She could still open the door and someone could be waiting to harm her.

But she wasn't hanging back for the rest of her life. This wasn't the first time she'd been afraid. Every time a car pulled into her driveway, her nerves jumped and her heart beat crazily. She felt this way every time she heard a car.

And every time, she took deep breaths and did what she was going to do now: answer it.

This time was different; this time she wasn't alone.

She marched past him. "You can be my backup."

He caught up to her, the door a stride away, made of thick, dark-colored wood with a small, diamond-shaped window. "I'll check," he said and angled himself in front of her.

She felt another new emotion. A surge of anger. She could tell it was anger because as he bent to peer out the tiny window that was the perfect height for her eyes, she had to stop herself from lifting her leg up and kicking him in his behind.

A very nice-looking behind in tan slacks, but she wanted to kick it anyway.

He stepped to the side, his face impassive. "It's your cousin. It's safe. She's with another woman."

"My cousin?" she asked.

"Debbie. She's your mother's cousin."

"I met her. She didn't like me." Debbie's image flicked into her mind. A big woman, built like a refrigerator. She had brown hair and gray roots in short, tight curls. And she had looked at Nia with dislike. As if Nia were a bug she wanted to squish beneath her sensible, black leather shoes.

"Debbie won't mess with me," he said. "I'll open it."

"I will." Nia lunged for the handle, knowing one thing: she couldn't count on this man. He didn't believe that Bast could talk, not even when Bast told her correctly how many fingers he'd held up.

Nia may have forgotten a lot, but it seemed to her that the cat was more trustworthy than the man.

Without peering out the tiny window, she flung the door back.

Immediately she recognized her cousin. She also recognized the woman standing next to her, with hate stabbing out of her eyes. A woman Nia recognized not

23

from memory, but from images on the Internet.
Her sister.

FIVE

Not much freaked out Rob since his return to Miracle. But looking at these two women, like two sides of the coin – so alike yet so different – chilled him.

"Why should *you* get it all?" The tall woman standing next to Debbie radiated venom, like a porcupine with poisoned spines.

Rob stepped next to Nia, who'd turned quiet, her face blank. He could feel her closing into herself. If she were a clam, she'd be pulling the clam shell over her and locking it tightly.

Debbie's gaze darted to him, her eyes wide, an *oh shit* look on her face. The other woman didn't glance at him, not even to acknowledge his presence.

It was easy to see this woman was related to Debbie. She was the younger and taller beauty-queen version; Debbie was the dulled-by-years-and-bad-choices version. The younger woman wore full makeup, as if ready for a photo shoot, and her shiny, light-brown hair curled below her shoulders.

Using her extra inches like a weapon, she stepped forward and towered over Nia.

Rob had the sick feeling it wasn't the first time she'd done this with Nia.

He shifted closer to Nia, his arm brushing hers. His hard stare let the woman know he was Nia's protector.

Wisconsin was nothing like Afghanistan. Green surrounded him instead of hard, sandy roads. Coolness stroked his bare wrists and face instead of dry, pounding heat. The air smelled moist and the last time he was at Wegner's buying coffee and tomato seeds, he'd heard Linda Wegner complaining about pollen.

No one complained about pollen in Afghanistan. Especially not his buddies in the army. They talked about the days before their tour was over and they'd be heading home. They talked about what they'd do when they got back. What they'd eat. Who they'd call. Their moms and dads and their kids. Their girlfriends and their wives. And how they would take a bath, just lay their heads back and soak in it.

Now he just took showers. In the stall long enough to clean himself, then out. As if there were danger around the corner and he had to be diligent. Even in a small village in the state of Wisconsin, where beer, cheese, and Packers were king, danger still hovered. People still hated. People still used weapons of destruction. People still killed.

Now he knew he'd been right to be careful. He smelled danger. It came from the tall woman with the scent of jasmine and whatever the hell else was mixed in her perfume. A sweet smell soured by intense hate.

He could take care of himself. But this loathing was aimed at the woman next to him, as real and dangerous as an IUD.

In his mind Morrisey's face flickered for a second. Half a face, actually. The other half blown off. One eye staring. His blood and parts of his face splashed on Rob.

The air changed, too. No noise. As if the aftermath of the percussion shock wave that broke his ear drum and temporarily deafened him was still erupting through the air, over and over and over.

No.

Denial roared up inside him.

No. Hell no. Fuck no.

No no no no no.

He hadn't been able to save Morrisey.

Or T. J., his face about three shades browner than the damn harsh ground, his mouth open and his eyes staring.

Two good men. Two dead men. One on each side of him.

For eleven months he'd been asking himself, *Why me? Why was I the one who lived?*

Noise rushed back as the reason swept into his mind, as clear as if he could see the words. This was why. Nia.

He couldn't save the others, but he could save Nia.

Sureness filled him. Swelled him with air, with purpose. Hardened his muscles. Thickened his shoulders and his neck.

He would not let anything happen to her.

Maybe he wasn't in the army anymore, but he could protect her.

He could not let her die. If necessary, he would die first.

The thought made him step forward. The woman intent on intimidating Nia backed up, giving him a look that asked *Who the fuck are you?*

Your enemy. That's who the fuck I am.

"I'm Constable Ackerman," he said. "And your name is...?"

The woman straightened her spine until she stood an inch or two taller than him. With a sniff, she looked down her nose at Rob. He glanced down, past her red, scooped-neck top and white slacks, and saw she wore shoes with inch-thick soles and six-inch heels that actresses wore on red carpets and strippers on stage. He'd never before seen anyone wear shoes like this in Miracle.

For the first time since he returned home, he held back laughter. Jerry was going to be sorry as hell he missed this.

In a nervous voice, Debbie introduced him to Justine, no last name, telling him she was Nia's sister.

Rob raised his eyebrows at Debbie, and she shrank back slightly and glanced around, as if seeking a way out.

Too late. He'd known about Debbie's unhappiness because she didn't get the house and property. Hell, the whole village had known. But Miracle was like Las Vegas. The people in the village knew each other's dirty business. No need to spread their dirt to the rest of the world.

He stepped back to Nia's side. Justine turned to her again, ignoring Rob as if he were a speck of dusk. Her gaze speared Nia.

"What do you have to say for yourself?" she demanded.

"Why do you hate me?" Nia's voice was almost a whisper. "I can't remember."

"Oh, you're so good at that innocent look, but it's wasted on me." Justine's scathing glance snapped to Rob. Her eyes were a brighter green than Nia's. Greener and angrier. "My sister tried to ruin my marriage. She seduced my husband. She singlehandedly ruined our family's business." She swept her hand out in a wide gesture. "And what did she get for that?"

"Ran over," he said.

Justine's eyes flashed. "When I heard about her accident, I was happy. I laughed and I celebrated."

"Did the police tell you it was no accident?"

"So? I didn't run her over. My husband and I were back together by then. Nia meant nothing to me, and she still doesn't." Justine skewered a look of hatred at Nia that made her words a lie. Her appearance at Nia's doorstep reinforced the lie. She seethed hatred. She stank of it. It streamed from the pores of her skin like poisonous gas.

Her lips pulled back in a sneer. "Maybe it was one of the other men she seduced then dumped."

"Yeah, I can see that she's a regular Siren," he said.

Justine's cheeks blotched. This close, Rob could see small signs that she was older than him. Little things he might not have noticed except for her layers of makeup. Though her skin was mostly unlined, a coarseness had begun.

Something brushed his legs and he glanced down. The cat.

Justine shifted her feet, and he looked up to see her make an offensive gesture at Nia. One that said *You are mud beneath my expensive stripper shoes*.

"The person you see here isn't the real Nia." Justine's upper lip curled in a sneer. "She lost weight, someone chopped off her hair, and she looks like a novice nun. This is all an act. Put on some makeup, a pushup bra and heels, and you won't recognize her."

"I recognize jealousy when I see it."

"You're wrong. It's not jealousy I feel, it's disgust." A drop of spit shone on Justine's lower lip as she narrowed her eyes at Nia. "I look at you and see dirt." Her voice vibrated with hate. "You were dirt when you were young. Never like the rest of us. And you're dirt now."

Rob felt Nia's stillness. Her watchfulness. He had the sense that he could see this woman through Nia's eyes. A creature from a fairytale. The evil queen, swooping down to destroy anyone who got in her way. Ready to wave her magic wand at anyone who possessed what she thought was hers and poof them into nothingness.

If Justine were the evil queen, Nia was one of the fairy tale princesses. Except for her cat, alone and unprotected in the witch's house.

Justine's jewel-green eyes cut to him. "You don't believe me. She's got you under her spell already. Poor little misunderstood Nia." She spat out the words, and her lips pulled back from her teeth. A predator about to take a bite of a live victim. "You don't know the real Nia. She's a destroyer. She's been that way since she was a baby, with her constant crying, her tantrums, and her demands for attention."

Rob put his hand on Nia's shoulder. With her small bones, it felt thin and fragile, like a child's...but stiff and unbending like a woman's.

"You sound like you're reading lines from a bad play." His gaze on Justine's face, her chin held high, didn't waver. "You want to see a destroyer, look in the mirror."

SIX

J ustine's laughter battered Rob's ears like gunshot. "She's fooling you just like she fools all the men. I could give you a list of names to call and ask about her. Ask my mother and my father first. They'll tell you."

Without waiting for him to respond, she turned her glare to Nia, the muscles in her face rigid. "*You* know what you were like. What you're still like. This is just another act. You're the same brat you were when you were six and stole my Barbie dolls. And after I took them back, you beheaded them. You ruined them like you ruined everything."

Beneath Rob's hand, Nia trembled. He shifted his gaze to Debbie, who stared from one sister to the other with saucer eyes, no doubt storing every word in her mind, every look, so she could faithfully repeat it all as soon as she had the chance, word by ugly word.

And no doubt the gossipmongers were already gathering at Wegner's the way vultures smelled road kill. Smelling blood in the air.

The darkness, always so near, swirled above him. Coming closer, closer...

"Take her away," he said to Debbie. "We've heard enough."

She blinked and gave a little shake. As if waking out of a bad dream. Rob wished it were that easy.

"I'm not ready to go." Justine lifted her chin. Her

green eyes flashed hatred. "I'm just beginning."

Rob gripped Nia's shoulder more firmly. The darkness was so close he felt its coldness. Like evil breaths on his skin. Any second now, it would swoop down and envelope him. Smother him and anyone close to him.

Not now. Stay away. I need to help her.

He imagined the murky cloud stopped inches away, frozen in the air above him. Quickly, before it dropped again, he speared Justine with his gaze, giving her his concentrated attention as if she were an exotic snake. "Begin somewhere else."

"What if I don't?" She sneered. "What are you going to do? Arrest me?"

He reminded himself that he wasn't a constable. He was a former US Army Sergeant, with a medical disability and a settlement that allowed him to heal.

But none of that mattered. As long as he inhaled and exhaled, he would always defend and protect. It was what his friends died for. He wasn't letting T. J. and Morrisey die in vain.

And right now, this woman shivering beneath his hand like a newly hatched baby robin needed his protection.

"I'll give you one minute to leave, and then I'll show you what I can do."

"Jerry!" Debbie said, her voice a gasp. But it was a gasp of delight, her face and eyes bright as she stared at his hand on Nia's shoulder. He could practically see her storing everything in her mind so she could repeat the good stuff without having to exaggerate too much.

A movement from Justine caught Rob's attention. Her hand dug into the purse hanging at her left hip. "I'm not going anywhere," she said as Rob drew back from

Nia. He bunched his muscles, ready to grab the sister. "No cheap village cop is going to—"

A hiss was all the warning the cat gave as she sprang straight up in the air, her claws out, small and deadly.

Debbie and Justine both screamed. Justine stepped backward and tripped over her feet in their uber-high heels. She stumbled back. Items fell out of her purse and thumped onto the wooden porch.

Given Debbie's bulk and age, she reacted faster than Rob would've expected, her arm whipping out to catch Nia's sister. As she did, the cat landed on Justine's chest.

Bast stuck her claws into the exposed skin.

Justine's high-pitched shriek made Rob wince, even with his bad left ear. Debbie jerked her hand back to her side. Clearly not about to get scratched just to save her relative. Justine tumbled back, shrieking louder.

Her head smacked onto the porch, cutting her voice off mid-screech. The cat growled and reached out to slash her claws at Justine's face.

Rob lunged down, caught the cat around its belly and pulled it up just as the cat's claws touched Justine's cheek.

The cat *mrowed*, its indignant tone needing no feline interpreter. Neither did the claws that swiped the back of Rob's hand.

Pain burned his hand, but he held onto the fighting cat, not letting go. He didn't know what this cat might do next.

"Bast." Nia grabbed the cat. Her hair brushed Rob's chin as she whispered something into Bast's ear that stopped the flailing legs and hissing mouth. Without saying another word, Nia cradled the cat against her chest, then swiveled and hurried indoors.

"I'm bleeding!" Justine cried. "I'm bleeding!"

Rob stared at the items dropped on the concrete: keys, a cell phone, tissues, and something people didn't usually take on a visit to their kid sister.

A gun.

He bent forward, grabbed it, and glowered Nia's sister into whimpering silence. He turned his attention to Debbie. "I'll give you two minutes to get her the hell off the porch or I'm arresting both of you."

"I have a carry permit!" Justine said.

"Show it to me."

She pulled the scooped neck of her top up and used it to pat the blood seeping from scratches on her upper chest. "I'm hurt and you're making me do this?"

He nodded at Debbie. "Either you do it, or I'm taking you in."

"You're disgusting."

He crossed his arms. "I'll give you one minute."

Debbie handed her the purse, then bent to pick up items from the porch. She oozed anger and dissatisfaction, her movements slow for a woman in her fifties.

Justine held her purse against her stomach. "This is ridiculous." She gave him a look that should have scorched the hair off his head. He touched it, to make sure it was still there, as long as Jerry's. No need for a military cut any more.

Those days were over. Or so he'd thought. Just the nightmares and the dark clouds remaining. Otherwise, he'd gotten off lightly with a ruptured eardrum and the constant *Why me?* question that kept whispering in his mind like a stupid, running track he couldn't turn off.

Justine bent her head to dig into her purse. It only took her seconds to come up with the card. "Here." She thrust it at him.

He looked at it then handed it back. "It's for Minnesota. You're in Wisconsin now."

"I forgot." Her voice was flat. "Give me my gun back." She glared. "I wasn't going to shoot Nia. I'm not crazy."

He handed her the card but not the gun. "I think you are a little crazy."

As she gasped, he turned and stomped inside, still holding the gun. With his retreat, Justine screamed at him, calling him a bastard. Hysteria in her voice. No control. A woman teetering past the verge of a breakdown, about to fall down fast and hard.

He didn't care. Let her fall into tiny pieces, and he still wouldn't care.

Just so she didn't take Nia down with her.

The door clattered shut behind him, muffling Justine's screeches. As he headed down the hall, he took out his cell phone and called his brother.

The phone rang on Jerry's end as he found Nia in the old-fashioned kitchen. The floor was black-and-white tiles, the counter was old-fashioned Formica, white with a gray stencil-like pattern, not even pretending to be granite or quartz or any expensive stone. In the corner with a toaster and a microwave on the counter behind her, Nia held the cat.

Murmuring to the cat, Nia tracked him with her gray-green eyes. Her words were too soft for Rob to hear, but his skin prickled.

Why was it he felt as if she were whispering a spell on someone?

On him?

He stopped just inside the kitchen, still waiting for Jerry to answer the damn phone.

Above him, the cloud lowered. Cold tendrils of dark air coiled around him, as if they were part of her murmuring spell.

The phone clicked, then Jerry's voice spoke in Rob's ear, telling him to leave a message. He waited for the beep. "Where the hell are you?" he demanded, mentally pushing away the dark tendrils that wanted to cling to him, to claim him. "I'm at Miriam's old house. There was an attack on the new owner by her sister. The sister had a gun, and I suspect she was going to use it. I've got the gun now, so get your ass over here."

Later he would crawl into his dark place. Right now Nia needed him.

SEVEN

The late morning sun streamed through the kitchen window and spotlighted the thin man striding toward Nia, his expression resolute.

Nia wondered if she'd known Rob before today. Not before she arrived in Miracle, but before the hospital. Before the memory loss.

He *felt* familiar. Not in her mind, but in her chest. In her skin. Even the hair on her head bristled with recognition.

Watching him, her heart thumped, too fast and too loud. His face wasn't beautiful, but he shone. Glimmered. Around him, sunlight sparkled. He was like a knight in shining armor, though she knew there was no such person. Not anymore. Maybe there never was.

Bast meowed her complaint at Nia's inattention, indignation in her voice. Informing Nia that Rob hadn't leapt at her sister. Bast had done that. Bast had stuck her claws into the sister's chest. And if *that man* hadn't stopped her, Bast would've scratched her face, too.

Nia bent her head to tell Bast how brave she was, but before she could speak, the cat's claws dug through her cotton sleeve and into the flesh of Nia's upper arm. The pain startled Nia, and she jerked back. Squealing, Bast sprang out of her grip and arced onto the maple floor.

As Bast darted out of the kitchen, Nia turned to watch Rob march toward her, his face tense, his gaze fixed on her. And somehow she knew, *she knew*, deep down in her damaged mind, that everything that happened since she'd found out about her inheritance and the village of Miracle had led to this moment.

He stopped in front of her. "I'll protect you."

"I don't need protection." She wanted to step toward him, like a dream sequence from a TV show. But this was no dream. She wasn't the heroine. He wasn't the hero.

Her cat was the hero.

He was still a liar.

And so was she.

She stayed where she was, her feet in her slip-on shoes planted on the floor, rooting her in place.

His cell phone burst out with guitar music, then a man with a southern accent sang to a girl that he was a real good man. Still looking at her in a way that made her go hot and cold and shiver, Rob lifted the phone to his ear. With Nia's sharp hearing, she heard the voice on the other end. It was a man's voice. Similar to Rob's, as if he spoke through a tin can. Even so, she had no problem making out the words.

"What the hell is going on?"

Rob raked his fingers through his hair. "You got a constable call. A possible intruder. I couldn't get hold of you, so I answered it. Where the hell are you?"

"Never mind. I'm on the way. Did you catch the intruder? Was it the sister?"

"I don't know. That was last night, and Nia sensibly didn't go out to check."

"Nia's the skinny chick with the bashed in brain, right? Slouches? Looks like she needs one of Rosa's lasagnas?"

"Hell, I need one of Rosa's lasagnas. Just get your ass over here. I think she might call the sheriff."

"The skinny chick?"

"Her name is Nia. You call her Miss Beaudine." Rob looked straight at her, into her eyes, and she knew he remembered what she said about her hearing and was wondering if she could hear every word his twin said.

"Ha-ha. I think you like her."

"She's not the one who might call the sheriff." He didn't lower his gaze. Somehow, it seemed...intimate. Making her skin shiver. "It's the other one," he continued. "The sister with the gun. She didn't pull it out, but her hand was in the purse when she, uh, slipped, and the gun fell out."

"Well, shit. And what do you mean by 'uh, slipped?'"

"Nia's cat jumped on her and scratched her face."

The real constable laughed. Rob grimaced, the expression on his face letting Nia know he wasn't happy with his brother any more than she was with her sister.

But it wasn't the same. Not the same at all. Her sister was a stranger to her. One who might or might not have come to her house intending to kill her.

"It's the gun that's important," Rob said. "I can't prove she was going to use it. She has a carry permit, but it's from Minnesota. I kept the gun, and she was screaming at me. She came with Debbie Gessner. They're probably at Debbie's house now. Get your ass over here and deal with it."

"I'm almost there. Make up an excuse to get out, so she won't catch us together."

"Nia already knows I'm not you." A side of his lips kicked up, but there was no humor in his face. His mournful eyes matched the sad that settled inside her chest and flowed through her veins.

"Fuck. You told her."

"I didn't tell her anything. She told me." He stared at

her. "She may have brain damage, but I think she's the smartest person I know."

Nia's breath slowed and goose bumps raced up and down her spine.

"You like her. I can tell."

"Just get over here." Rob hung up. He set the phone on the counter, still staring at her. As if afraid that if his gaze wavered – if he even blinked – she would zap away.

She kept staring back. Noticing his brown irises were rimmed with navy blue. His nose wasn't a smooth blade like she'd thought; it had a little bump. His eyebrows were lush.

It made her wonder what else about him was lush.

Made her chest tighten.

These thoughts...these feelings...were new to her. She wasn't sure if she liked them. They made her head feel funny. Everything in her body felt funny.

"She's going to tell the sheriff about me," she said, and her voice sounded odd. As if she'd swallowed smoke.

"You weren't doing anything wrong. She came to your house with a gun, and without a Wisconsin permit. She's the one who broke the law."

"She hates me." Nia crossed her arms. She didn't know how to handle any of this: her sister and all the hate she brought with her, and this man, with more emotion.

Nia wanted it to stop. All of it. She wanted it to go away. "Dr. Whitcomb told me that because so many of my brain cells were destroyed, I'm essentially a different person than I was before someone ran over me with their car."

"What person was that?" He took a step toward her.

Her heartbeat sped. If it had tires, he'd be giving her a speeding ticket. "You heard her. A liar. A bad person."

"Just because she said it doesn't make it true. She could be the liar. She didn't seem sane to me."

"She's not the only one. Everyone in my family said it." She frowned because she was lying. And she'd told herself she wouldn't lie anymore. It was true that omission wasn't a lie. Not when it was an accident.

But when it was on purpose...

"Almost everyone," she said.

He stopped, his forehead crunched. "I think..." His lips pressed together and he shook his head, frowning so hard the skin pulled on his forehead. "Something she said bothers me. But it doesn't matter. What matters is that she came to your house unprovoked and uninvited, with a gun in her purse. Her animosity must've been building up inside her for a long time."

She nodded, but inside she felt a deep sadness. Deep as the middle of Miracle Lake. "Debbie doesn't like me, either. I don't know what I did to her before this."

"Debbie was Miriam's only relative who lived in Miracle. She expected to inherit the house."

"She's mad because of the house?"

"And the money."

"Without the money, I'd have to work." Nia spoke slowly, because they were words she didn't want to say. But the idea forming in her mind was the right thing to do.

She'd messed up the first part of her life, doing the wrong thing every chance she had. She knew that because of the letters. This part, she wanted to do things the right way.

The left side of her head itched, but she scratched the right side. "I don't have a lot of money. Because of my...brain problems, a lawyer appointed by the court is taking care of my money. It's invested so I can use so much a month. I don't think they would let me give it away. But I could let Debbie have a room here."

"Don't." His voice was hard and so were his eyes and his mouth. The hardness of a man certain he was right. "Debbie is your enemy. Keep your enemy out of your house. Miriam didn't owe Debbie anything. Neither do you."

She looked into his eyes. "I want to do the right thing."

"The right thing to do is to protect yourself. An enemy in your house is worse than a live bomb."

She frowned. Was he right? Or maybe he didn't like people.

She'd discovered from TV and from real life that people made decisions with their emotions, not their minds.

People were confusing.

"If you don't care about yourself," he went on, "at least protect your cat. You want someone who resents you to be anywhere near the cat you love?"

She went cold. Frozen. Then a rush of alarm shot through her.

If Bast was hurt, it would feel like someone tore her lungs out of her chest. "No," she said, and her voice quavered. "Never. I'll remember that."

In his hard face, his lips softened. "Whatever they said about you is wrong." His voice was soft, too. Tender. Like her voice when she talked to Bast sometimes, when Bast was kneading her lap and purring like a toy train. "You're a good person. Too good."

She felt a glow inside her even as she shook her head. "I'm trying to make up for the things I did wrong before. This time around, I'm trying to be better."

"You can't believe anything Justine said."

"She's my sister."

"She didn't act sisterly."

"Every person she mentioned said the same thing in their letters to me."

As if he'd been hit by lightning, his body froze. His brown eyes blazed. "*That's* what I wanted to talk to you about. The letters."

She nodded even as she cringed inside. A hard twist in her belly that came every time she thought of the letters.

They haunted her. The ugly words of all the ugly things she'd done were seared into her brain.

A car turned into her driveway, small stones crunching under the tires, but she ignored it, her attention on Rob as he took another step toward her.

"Do you have them here?" He looked to the side, and she knew he heard the car cruise to the back of the house instead of in front. He started toward the back door. "We'll talk about the letters later. I hope to hell that's Jerry."

She trailed after him. In her next session with Dr. Whitcomb, she was going to have a lot more than usual to tell him.

EIGHT

Watching Jerry saunter along the path bordered with red and yellow tulips – as if he were on a damn nature walk – Rob wanted to sock him in the chin that looked just as stubborn as his.

He pulled back the door and scowled. "Are you done with your stroll through the tulips? You ready to come in and change? What do you wanna bet her sister is calling the sheriff already? Or a lawyer?"

"You can check the sheriff off your list. I called and let them know what happened. They're not touching it."

"No shit. You're always whining that the sheriff wants to bust into your business. Why isn't he jumping to get into this?"

"I think it was the mention of the cat and the two sisters." Jerry grinned. "Remember Dennis Ladke? Two grades ahead of us in school?"

"With the Dumbo ears?" Rob stepped back and let his brother in. He glanced at the box beneath Jerry's arm, taped and with a mail label on it.

"He's a deputy now." Jerry's grin widened. "He said they didn't want to get in the middle of no damn cat fight."

"Yeah, but this was a cat fight with a gun."

"It's my guess the sister wouldn't mention the gun." Jerry looked past him at Nia. Immediately, his eyes changed and he stood taller. Smiled like he wanted to dazzle her. If he had tail feathers, like a peacock, he'd be strutting in front of her with his feathers unfurled in full display.

Rob flicked his gaze to her. From the stony way she regarded Jerry, Rob guessed she was remembering Jerry calling her a skinny, slouching chick.

"Besides, fishing season opened," Jerry said. "The ATV trails are open. Drunks are out. That's keeping the deputies busy without interfering in a sister fight." He turned back to Nia. "We met before but you might not recall. I'm Jerry Ackerman. The real law in this village. My apologies for not being here when you needed me."

"No apologies needed." She glanced at Rob. "Your brother did just fine."

Rob felt his chest swelling like there was a balloon inside him blowing up, helium gone wild. "I've got an idea," he said. "A big idea."

She tilted her head. "What?"

"I'll have to read the letters first."

Her face closed. "No," she said. "No."

He nodded, even as he thought, yes, you will.

"You know what they say in stories about murder mysteries," Jerry said.

They both looked at him.

"When a gun is introduced, it needs to be used."

Nia frowned and blinked. Rob crossed his arms and glared at Jerry. That was just like Jerry. Being his usual jerky self and not caring that he was upsetting Nia. "But what if it's a red herring?"

"There's no herring in this part of the state, red or otherwise. Just good old Wisconsin bass."

"Real funny. Lucky for you, no one's paying you for your jokes."

"Or your brains."

Rob glared at him. "You're the constable. What do you want to do with the gun?"

"Give it back. And don't give me any crap about it. Like it or not, it's the law. Wisconsin honors concealed carry gun permits from Minnesota."

"At least take the bullets out."

Jerry shook his head. "Can't do that. Legally, she can keep the bullets in her gun. Besides, it's easy enough to buy more bullets and come back."

Darkness settled inside Rob's chest, tendrils of the cloud winding around his heart.

He turned back to Nia. "Just to make sure she doesn't come back with the gun, I'm staying here with you."

"In that case..." Jerry turned to Nia and held out the box he was still carrying. "Nia will likely be bored, and it's a good thing I brought this."

"Brought what?" Rob glared at the package, a rectangular box. He recognized the label. "Is that a book?"

"I didn't open it, but that's my guess." Jerry still held it out to Nia, who shook her head and put her hands behind her, looking at the package as if it held a bomb.

Rob's protective instincts rushed to attention. "What is it?" He stepped in front of her. It wasn't likely someone sent her an explosive through the United States Postal Service, but stranger things – and even more horrible things – had happened.

And if another bomb went off in Rob's vicinity, he wasn't going to look to his side and see someone else dead. He didn't want to die, but if anyone was killed in this house in the next moment, he knew one thing: it wasn't going to be Nia.

"What the hell is it?" he repeated.

She laughed but it was shaky. The kind of laugh

someone made when they really wanted to cry.

He knew about those laughs. It was always a choice: either laugh or take out his gun and start shooting.

"I think it's just a book," Nia said. But she gazed at him out of eyes that looked bruised.

"That must be a hell of a book," Jerry said with a drawl.

Rob held out his hands. "Give it to me."

NINE

Nia groaned as Jerry frowned at the box, not giving it to Rob.

When would she learn to do anything right? It *was* just a book. Just like she said. From the same online retailer as the other two times in the same size package.

Thousands of packages like this went out every day. Maybe millions. Traveling across the United States. Traveling across other countries, too. Going straight from computer to warehouse to residence or perhaps post office box.

She imagined most of the items were received with smiles and squeals. Maybe a few recipients would scratch behind their ears and look at the boxes with puzzled foreheads. Not expecting it. Wondering who was sending it to them.

But this fear squeezed her lungs tight, her breathing restricted, as if a wolf were in the package, ready to spring out...

When she knew what was in the package. Knew it wasn't a wolf.

It didn't matter. Didn't stop her speeding heartbeat. She didn't know where this fear came from. She just wished it would stop. It burned through her veins like poison instead of blood.

Looking at the box, she put her hands behind her

back and clasped them, as if it were Pandora's Box. She'd learned about the myth on History Channel. Pandora opened the box, and the evils of the world flew out.

But that wasn't true. Even with her damaged brain, she was aware that the evils of the world were already out there.

And so were the wonders.

That was the real reason she wandered around town. Besides watching to see the way people behaved so she could learn how to mimic them.

But better than seeing how people acted were the animals darting through the yards. The squirrels flying from branch to branch. The mama birds leading Nia away from their baby birds. Protecting them.

The flowers budding.

The grass turning green.

Watching the earth come alive this spring had made her imagine she was watching the beginning of creation, even more beautiful than the sunrise or a rainbow. Almost as beautiful as the morning she'd seen a deer, a cardinal, and a blue bird.

Almost as beautiful as the first time she'd seen Bast. A tortoiseshell cat, the vet told her later, in shades of black, gray, and white, with the markings of a small tiger. So magnificent, Nia's breath had stopped in her lungs and she'd had put her hands together and bowed down to the cat.

She held onto that feeling now. The glory of life instead of the ugliness.

"What are you thinking?" Jerry asked.

She blinked. Able to breathe again with no trouble. The burn in her veins gone.

"That I need to stop thinking so much." She stepped next to Rob. Held her hands out to Jerry. "I'll take it. I've gotten this twice before. It's nothing horrid. Just a book."

"You didn't act like it was a book," Rob said.

She glanced at him. "I don't act like normal people about anything. I'm learning."

"You seemed afraid of the book. Are you afraid of everything?"

"Afraid is the wrong word." She spoke slowly because her mind was moving slowly, sorting through words to find the correct one. Thousands of words. Did the world need so many? "I'm cautious."

"Of everything?" Rob asked.

"Not of you."

His pupils narrowed. The muscles in his face tensed. He stared at her as if he were memorizing the shape of her eyes. The way her bangs clung to her forehead. The way she held her head high. According to Dr. Whitcomb, who taught classes in body language, she was daring anyone to criticize her.

Jerry laughed, low in his throat. But she and Rob continued to stare at each other. Neither blinking. Like a game Nia played with Bast and only won when Bast didn't care.

Jerry's chuckle faded, as if the volume was turned down. As if all there were in this world was Rob and her. And she could only hear his heartbeat and he could only hear hers and nothing else.

"You want the package or not?" Jerry asked.

She felt as if she were in a dream. Not an unusual feeling. At least this time it wasn't turning into a nightmare.

"Yes," she said.

"Give it to me," Rob said.

Jerry grinned and gave it to her.

Triumph leapt inside her. Then she looked at the

package in her hands, and the triumph crumbled into an unrecognizable swarm of feelings. She could open up a dictionary of emotions, and everything she felt would be in it, making one big emotion soup.

"What are you going to do now?" Rob asked.

"What do you think she's going to do?" Jerry's voice held laughter. "She's going to open it."

She looked up at him, and he nodded, a wide grin on his face that looked so much like Rob's, and yet so different.

"I know what you're thinking," Jerry said, "and you're right. I am the smart twin."

Jerry made her laugh.

But Rob made her heart feel...safe.

Sometimes it seemed to Nia that life was a war; other times life was a comedy. Now she was sure it was the first as Rob took a deliberate step toward his brother, his arm drawn back to punch him.

Nia's breath stopped, her eyes wide, her heart hammering. She held the package against her chest, feeling the thick cardboard and the sharp corners. Her mind saying *oh no, oh no, oh no.* Over and over. A wordless, desperate plea that it wouldn't happen.

Except it was happening. She watched, unable to look away. Unable to stop it. Disaster inevitable. Rob's fist rushed forward, his knuckles slamming into Jerry's shoulder.

Jerry's upper body jerked back and then up again. He said "Ouch!" But even as the word came out, he grinned, and he even added a laugh.

Expecting the worst, Nia stared for a second before she understood that the worst wasn't happening. They never planned to hurt one another. They were like families on TV that way. The kind that said bad things to each other and then laughed.

Her hands shook as she turned away from them to the counter. Sick to her stomach.

A step came after her.

"What are you doing?" Rob asked, his voice wrapping around her, warm with concern.

A comfort voice, she thought. She liked his voice. She liked a lot about him.

Grabbing that thought, she held it close to her as she reached for the wooden block on the countertop and pulled out a knife. As she sliced open the tape on the box, she held the comfort of his voice to her even tighter.

You'll be okay. You'll be okay.

After all, she knew what was going to happen.

A moment later, she pulled out the oversized book: *Harry Potter and the Prisoner of Azkaban* by J.K. Rowling.

Why? she asked. Just as she'd done the other two times.

Who? she asked this third time.

Just like the other two times, a gaping silence answered her. She picked up the paperwork, scanning it. Aware that both men were watching her. Feeling the heat from Rob as he stood too close.

She didn't tell him to back up. His nearness reassured her. It made her feel...protected.

He was not going to let anyone harm her.

"You got this from Patty?" Rob demanded, his voice sharp. And she knew he was talking not to her but to his brother about the lady who delivered her mail. She knew because he didn't talk to her in a voice that could be used to slice a tough cut of meat.

"Patty was reaching the driveway when I pulled in," Jerry said, surprising her because his tone was serious and he wasn't joking.

On TV, men said things to make themselves look good. Or bad. The ruder they were, the more laughs they got.

Maybe that was part of the reason she'd stayed away from men.

The other part was that there was a fifty percent chance that the person who tried to kill her was a man.

She still stared at the book, all the thoughts swirling around her mind, like invisible letters twirling in an air funnel. But the only letters that mattered were in the book filled with words and all the wonderfulness that was Harry and his world.

"You know who sent it?" Rob asked.

She shook her head. Before he could ask, she said, "And I don't know why."

"Does Harry Potter mean anything to you?"

She shook her head. "His name is familiar. I think I heard it before I left the hospital, but I don't know when or where. Maybe one of the therapists or nurses. Maybe the doctors." Or the aides or the cleaning people. It could have been anyone.

"Mind if I look in the box?" Jerry asked, already pulling it from her.

She shook her head but he'd taken it already. Instead of the box, she looked at the cover with the boy on it and the Z on his forehead.

If there were a letter on her forehead, it would be *E* for Empty to describe her brain.

Or *B* for Befuddled.

Or *FS* for Feeling Stupid.

From what she'd seen in her house and in the whole

village, she'd have to fight other people for the *FS*.

"I read the books," Rob said.

She looked up sharply, feeling surprise. She hadn't thought of him as someone who would read fiction. Especially about a boy who was mistreated by his uncle and turned out to be a wizard with a powerful and evil wizard trying to kill him and his friends.

"Rob's the reader." Affection and maybe a little pride warmed Jerry's voice that was similar in tone and inflection to Rob's.

Nia suspected that anyone else with their back to the two men might not know which one was talking. To her they were as different as a cat from a dog.

"What about you?" she asked.

"I'm the lover." Jerry grinned, holding one of the papers from the box. Then his lips straightened into grimness. His gaze shifted to hers. "You're right. There's no name saying who sent this. You should call the store and demand to know the name of the gift giver."

She shook her head. "I did last time. They said if it were something offensive, they might send the purchaser a warning."

"It's offensive to me," Rob said. "If it makes you uneasy, I don't like it."

"I don't think it does. They make me happy, but not knowing who sent them makes me wonder if..." Her voice lowered to a whisper and stopped. She didn't want to say she wondered whether someone might care about her. That was too pathetic. Instead she stared at the book in her hands. Her fingertips prickled. She wanted badly to read it. To linger over every page and share with her cat and—

Her breath stopped. Bast used to sleep through her readings. Not concerned that her voice was breathless with the thrill and concern she felt for Harry, Ron, and Hermione. Their victories giving her hope...

But almost always, each victory came with death and destruction...with the conviction that in the next book, worse was on the way.

Was that what her life was about? Was there worse coming her way?

"Have you read all the books?" Jerry asked.

She shook her head.

"They're at the library. The series is done. The movies are out."

"I know." She looked at him finally, and saw the frown on his forehead as if he were trying to make up his mind about her. He saw her weirdness and wanted to put it in a category. One that said *Too Weird To Handle.* Or another that said *Weird, But Nothing Weirder Than Just About Anyone Else I Know.*

After all, they lived in the village of Miracle, where just two weeks ago, a message was left on car windows in a church parking lot, prophesying that a miracle was coming.

She glanced at the face behind his. Rob. He frowned, too. The kind of frown that said he cared for her. And she didn't see a label in his eyes.

That couldn't be right. Everyone had a label for everyone else. One that said brother, mother, daughter, alcoholic, sexaholic, control freak, loser, winner, hunter, bowler, cook...and on and on and on. If there were one thing the world wasn't short of, it was labels.

"This isn't the first one," Rob said.

"It's the third."

"You have the other two?"

She heard the patience in his voice. Not patience for effect but real patience. Asking questions because the answers might give him the key to the secret.

But she'd thought and thought and thought about it...and she didn't know the secret.

"They were sent to me, too. I've gotten them about a month apart."

"Can you think of a reason?"

She shook her head. "I don't see a reason for a lot of things in life."

"What do you see a reason for?" Jerry asked, and in his voice she heard amusement. And curiosity. The desire to fit her in a category again.

She looked past him at Rob.

And the thought came to her that looking at Rob's serious face was a good reason for being alive.

With her heart beating differently – a little faster, a little happier – she shifter her gaze to Jerry.

"I'm not the person you should ask that question."

"Who should I ask?"

She shook her head. Was that a serious question? Did he have a therapist? But she wasn't sure if her therapist was much help to her. And she didn't think most villagers would go to one.

"Your minister?" she asked.

He cracked a hard laugh.

She shot a look back at Rob. "Our minister's wife just left him," he said, "and Jim just announced that he was cheating on her."

"Jim's the pastor," Jerry said. "I wasn't surprised to hear it."

"Me neither," Rob said.

"Our mom was shocked, though," Jerry said.

"She has faith."

"Yeah." Jerry sounded glum.

Rob nodded, and he looked glum, too, and Nia

wondered why. Wasn't faith a good thing?

Normal people were...odd. Thinking about them made her head ache.

"I'll put this with the others. No need to come with me." She gathered the box and the papers, then hurried out of the kitchen. Behind her she heard silence, and then the padding of four feet.

She raced up the steps, feeling as if she were running from a monster creeping out from under the bed.

Only the monster wasn't the two men, it wasn't Bast, it wasn't the book. It was a whispery, sibilant evil that wanted to destroy her...but she couldn't remember who or what it was.

She only knew that it had left her alone for a while...

And now it was back.

TEN

Her predator instincts on alert, Bast followed the two men to the back office where they decided to exchange clothes to spare Nia the sight of their unclothed bodies.

Humans were odd that way. As if they didn't all have the same equipment, with only a few changes according to their sex.

She felt pity and disdain for humans. Their clothes never made up for being furless. At the most they had only a few puny hairs that left too much skin exposed and wouldn't protect their bodies from the burning sun in summer and the blustery, stinging winds in winter.

Not like cats with thick fur that protected them from the weather, and made them lovely to look at and soft to touch.

Bast padded into the office behind Jerry. He closed the door, and it brushed her tail. She whisked her tail up, then she made herself small in the corner of the room.

She wanted to be with Nia, but danger was in the air. Bast smelled it, as if the air was charged with storm warnings.

Like all great hunters, she was vigilant every day. Today she needed to be extra vigilant.

Men had invaded the house. Two men who looked the same but smelled so different.

Neither of them could protect Nia as well as she

could. If cats had thumbs, they would rule the world. Except for that one small but important thing, they were superior to humans in almost every way.

"You like her," Jerry said. His voice was almost the same as Rob's but lighter. As if he carried less weight on his shoulders. "I can tell. You really like her."

Bast stared at him. Of course he could tell what was going on. Nia's scent had changed since this morning, her body sending out smells that said it was ready for breeding. Even Jerry with his puny human powers of scent must smell it.

Men had their breeding scents, too. The ones that said they would make a strong baby with big lungs and a healthy body. A baby that would grow strong and prosper. A baby that would be smart in the ways of the world and would thrive.

Both men were sending out that scent.

But in this house at least, Rob's was stronger.

Mating season had begun.

The time when humans acted more stupid than usual.

"It's none of your damn business who I like," Rob said. "I don't stick my nose into your business and ask where you are at night or who she is."

"I can understand you're cranky." Jerry's voice mocked him. So did his lips, twisting up on one side. "I hear that abstinence does that to a guy. Normally I'd be glad you're showing an interest in any woman, but this one's got some serious issues."

Bast hissed, but Jerry's harsh laughter covered her voice. He pulled his zipper up, and it made a sound that imitated her hiss but could never equal it. Humans could never equal a cat in so many ways.

"You may not have noticed," Rob said, "but I've got serious issues, too."

"You've always had serious issues. Nothing new with that." The two men switched clothes, moving quickly while Bast studied their bodies to see if they would be appropriate mates for Nia.

It was hard because they looked so alike. But with the scents curling through the air, Bast knew someone had to watch out for Nia. She wasn't like most humans, but when the time came for animals to mate, all of them, human or feline, listened to their bodies instead of their brains.

Lucky for Nia she had Bast to watch out for her.

Jerry and Rob finished changing clothes then stepped into the hall, Jerry first, carrying the gun that had fallen out of Nia's sister's purse. Bast padded after Rob, watching to see what they would do. She didn't want to miss anything.

"Damn it, Jerry. You're really going to give it back to her?"

Jerry looked over his shoulder at Rob. "There's nothing illegal about it."

"At least take the bullets out. Tell her there were none in when you got it."

Facing Rob, Jerry crossed his arms, still holding the gun. "She'll just buy more."

"You want to see Nia killed?"

"Don't worry. After I get through with the sister, she won't want to kill anyone."

"You planning on charming her into giving up her plans to kill Nia?"

"Remember what Mom used to say about honey catching flies?"

"Justine's no fly. She's a wasp. Before you go to Debbie's, stop by the farm. I'm sure Mom has wasp spray left over from last year."

Jerry shook his head. "Give me a little trust, will ya? I gotta do what I gotta do, and you gotta do what you gotta do."

For a long moment the two men stared at each other. Then Rob shrugged. "Mom always said you had a head like cement."

"She always said the same thing about you."

"Yeah, but she didn't say my brains rattled like marbles in a can. Do what you think you've got to do. I'm staying with Nia until I'm sure she's safe."

Jerry's smile flashed and he uncrossed his arms. "And I'll take care of her sister."

"The sister might be gone." Rob's face brightened. "Maybe she left already. I hear there's going to be a full moon soon. She could be driving back to her coven."

"Not without her gun. From what you said, she's not the kind of woman who's going to leave home without it."

Rob groaned. "You should be arrested for bad punning."

Jerry gave him an insulting hand gesture that didn't need interpretation and headed for the kitchen door, his steps purposeful.

Bast prowled after him. She didn't trust either man, but more than the two men, she didn't trust Nia's sister.

This might be the perfect chance to find out what Justine was up to.

ELEVEN

The attic was as crowded with the past as Nia's mind was empty of it: old furniture, boxes, and trunks.

The place even smelled old. Unused. Someone else's memories. Taking up room in Nia's house while she searched for her own.

Standing on the threshold, she listened to the growl of an engine from outside as Jerry's car pulled out of the driveway. He was gone, but she remained still. Breathing shallowly and lightly. Listening and waiting.

Sure enough, in another second footsteps clomped up the stairs.

In that second, she breathed deeper. In that instant, the musty and dusty attic seemed brighter and the air clearer.

She stepped into the attic, barely an inch shorter than the low door frame. The long room ran the length of the house. There was a pull chain by the door for lights, but it wasn't necessary. The grimy windows on the front and back of the room filtered in the sunlight, muting the rays so it looked like a place to film a rock video. She threaded her way between sheet-covered pieces of furniture and a few old trunks with boxes piled on top of them. Her mother's cousin and the ancestors who'd lived in the house before her hadn't been the type to throw much away.

Nia certainly didn't want to throw away anything now. She was afraid she'd get rid of something important and worthwhile.

Dr. Whitcomb had thought that was wise of her, but she suspected it was cowardice instead of wisdom. Prudence generated by fear.

She didn't want to live her life creeping around, watching others. She wanted to stride forward with boldness. To fight fear instead of holding back and peering around with bated breath. To live life loudly instead of lurking in silence.

She was halfway to the desk in the corner when a footstep stomped on the landing. Glancing behind her, she saw Rob ducking his head to step inside. When he straightened, it seemed to her that the room lit up even more. That this attic wasn't filled with stuff that needed to be thrown out, but remnants of lives. Beautiful in its way.

And so was he.

Yet she felt a sudden desire to flee.

Of course the change in the atmosphere was her imagination. Dr. Whitcomb said her thoughts formed her world, so no wonder everything in her world seemed crooked. Her brain was lopsided with missing parts, and that's how she saw the world. Especially the village of Miracle, where strange was normal. A place where people – and pets – acted inappropriately.

And she'd heard whispers that magical things happened, too.

That people expected miracles, just as it had been prophesied.

But that was silly. Miracles didn't happen. Nia didn't know a lot, but she knew that much. The only miracles that happened were with magicians using magic tricks.

According to Dr. Whitcomb, people thought miracles happened because it made them feel good. And the village was named Miracle, and maybe that's why so many of them believed it.

Though not everything in Miracle made people feel good. Miracle wasn't...normal. Not that she was sure what normal was, but she was already sure that Miracle wasn't it. Unless normal was crafted out of children's clay by a giggling Queen of Hearts from Alice in Wonderland, yelling "Off with her head."

Her sister wanted to say that to her. So maybe she fit right in.

After all, she was the only one whose cat talked to her.

As far as she knew.

"Are the books here?" Rob asked. He wore the jeans and black T-shirt that Jerry had been wearing earlier, but she didn't have any doubt that it was him and not his identical twin. Just something about his expression, a seriousness his brother lacked. Or maybe it was the way he looked at her. The intensity in his brown eyes that made her heart beat faster and her skin heat from the inside out.

"They're in the backroom downstairs," she said. "On the bookshelf."

His eyebrows rose.

"They're just books." She lifted her chin, feeling oddly defensive.

"So you read the other two?"

Read? As in devoured? She nodded. She hadn't told Dr. Whitcomb about the books and her reaction to them, the kinship she felt for the orphaned Harry Potter.

That sense of kinship was because of the letters, she knew. Her family was like the Dursleys, mixed in with

Cinderella's stepmother and stepsisters.

Though according to them, she was the sister who was wicked.

"Why are you upset?" Rob asked.

"I told you to stay downstairs," she said and heard the quaver in her voice.

He glanced around. As if he knew how nervous she was and how she wanted to lock the attic door and climb up on the roof and stay there until he left.

"What's in here?" he asked. "If not the books, what are you looking for?"

"You asked about the letters. They're here."

His head lifted, and he looked straight at her. "Hidden?"

She shrugged and headed toward the front of the attic. Her progress disturbed the nearly still dust motes, and they did an odd dance in the air. She didn't know why she'd kept the letters. Why she'd shoved them in the old desk. It was like keeping a container of open poison in her house and hoping no one drank it.

"Is this all yours?" Rob asked.

"Nothing is mine." Maybe that's why she saved the letters. At least this was something of hers. A record of the person she was before the attempted murder, even if that person was evil.

She reached the desk below the rectangular window that probably hadn't been washed since decades before she was born. She slid open the desk drawer and her hand shook as she reached for the manila envelope.

A silent scream started in her head. Her stomach tightened. As if a snake in her belly coiled around her intestines. Tighter and tighter.

"Your stuff is downstairs then?" he asked.

"I came here with nothing. No clothes. No furniture.

65

No jewelry. Nothing."

"Everyone has something."

"They told me I had nothing."

"You sure the hell had *something*. Someone hasn't been taking care of you."

His voice was behind her now, and her skin shivered, as if the notes of his voice penetrated the layers and burrowed into her cells. She picked up the manila envelope with the poisonous letters, took a step back, and tossed it to him.

"I'm alive. That's all that mattered. Whatever belonged to the woman I was before..." She stopped and couldn't talk for an instant. But he kept watching her. Patient. As if he planned to wait hours for her to finish, if that's what it took. "I don't want anything she had."

He nodded and she realized his jaw was clenched and anger simmered in his eyes. Around her, she felt the still air thicken with his frown.

Already the letters were causing damage.

And he hadn't read them yet.

"Let's go downstairs," Nia said. "On the porch." It seemed to her that reading the letters on the big front porch would be less dangerous than in an enclosed room.

On the way down, she felt that something seemed missing. It wasn't until they were on the front porch that she realized what it was.

Bast. She must be napping somewhere, but as Nia sat on the cushioned rattan, three-cushion glider on the porch, she wished Bast were with her, her body warm on her lap, sending her love.

Bast wouldn't care how terrible she'd been in her last life.

All Bast cared was that Nia feed her, pet her, and love her. In return, Bast kept mice and rats away, warned her when intruders were in their yard, and most of all, she loved Nia back.

No wonder she hadn't felt the need for a man since she was released from the hospital.

Until now.

TWELVE

It was warm outside, but as Rob silently read the letters, he felt cold down to the soles of his feet and the marrow of his bones. On the crisp white paper used by all of them, as if someone had passed them out and ordered the others to write, the letters seemed to writhe snakelike. It was a trick of his mind, he knew, brought on by the contents. But that didn't take away any of the evil in their words. Nor did it didn't take away the sorrow he felt for Nia.

If it hurt him to read it, how much more would it hurt Nia?

No wonder she kept them in the dark attic.

He would've burned them. And then, when they were ashes, buried them. Or thrown them in the trash to take the poison far away from her.

With each sentence, the darkness that hovered near him thickened and lowered. A breathing, living, evil cloud. And he knew that it wasn't just near him. It was growing in width and depth, encroaching on Nia's space, breathing its poison at her, too.

A picture grew as he read the mother's first. It was the least cruel, Rob suspected, the reason Nia gave it to him first. Letting him tiptoe into the deep end of the poisoned pool of her family.

The mother apologized for not coming to see her since the accident, but the others in the family forced her to choose. She took the blame for whatever had made Nia into what she was. If she'd been home, maybe she could have taken the brunt of Nia's tantrums and found some help for her. But her income had always been needed. And Nia's father had been a better parent than she was. Much more patient during the difficult times. Still, she was sorry, she was sorry, she was oh so sorry.

Rob's teeth clenched. The mother said she was sorry, but not sorry enough to visit her severely injured daughter the hospital. Not sorry enough to raise her.

Nia jumped up and strode to the end of the porch. She hunched over the railing, her shoulders raised to cover her lower face, her long neck scrunched like a turtle, her arms on the top rail pressed close to her ribs below her breasts. She was closed in, protecting herself while waves of tension streamed from her.

Rob resisted an urge to head over to her, put his arms around her, and comfort her. After all, he didn't know her that well. They'd only met a few hours ago. Anything more was in his disturbed mind.

He reminded himself that he'd come here not out of altruistic notions or concern for her, but to protect his brother. To cover up for him.

And now he felt a compulsion to protect this woman.

A fierceness tensed his muscles, and he clenched his teeth to keep from crumpling the paper.

No one was going die on his watch again.

He sucked in a deep breath. One letter done. He slapped it on the rattan table next to the glider and unfolded the next letter.

This one covered two pages. He turned to the second page and his gaze slid down to the signature with the large, loopy letters and a blob over the I in the name Justine. J for jealous, he thought. The sister who came to visit with a surprise up her sleeve or, rather, in her purse. A gun.

Not the normal gift for a recovering sister. But the Beaudines weren't the normal family.

He turned back to the first page, which started with a complaint about the way Nia screamed as a baby so Justine couldn't sleep at night. As if Nia had deliberately cried to keep her awake. And then Nia's tantrums as she grew older. The screams. The way she broke things. The fits of anger. And later, the silences. The rudeness. The gloominess. And as a teen, the promiscuity...

Reading it, Rob grew cold.

It all sounded...familiar.

After he finished, he took the letter written by Justine's husband. This was typed in the same format as the other two, and another round of coldness wrapped around Rob's heart.

The husband blamed Nia for seducing him. Breaking up his marriage. Purposely going after him and then dropping him.

Sometime during this, she stole the list of their clients from his computer.

He frowned and read that paragraph twice before he realized Nia had worked as an agent at a rival real estate company, while Justine and her husband worked for her father.

The last letter was the most chilling. From her father who called her a chronic liar from early childhood. By the time Rob finished reading, the darkness dropped down and blanketed him. Swaddled him in iciness. Prickled him in heat. The sun shone brightly, but he read the words through a film of gray.

The silence stretched as he stared into the gray. Small, gasping breaths finally broke through the darkness to his ears. Nia's footsteps slapped on the porch, and she crossed in front of him to return to the house.

He reached up and grabbed her wrist. Her arm was trembling. He looked up at her face and saw fear and hurt and grief.

"Tell me," he said, hearing the rawness of his voice. A gruff whisper.

"I don't know anything." Her voice was even rawer.

"Maybe not with your brain. But you've known since you were a child."

"Known what?"

"That you were abused."

She crumpled. He stood to catch her and hold her close.

"I know," he whispered as she trembled in his arms. Her silent tears dampened his T-shirt. "I know what it's like to be afraid."

But what he'd known had been because of war. Not a member of his family.

THIRTEEN

Anger flared inside him. Red and hot and wanting to flame out. When he found out who did this— He damped the fury down. Another part of the darkness. He'd deal with it later. Maybe never, because Nia didn't need revenge, she needed healing. In order to heal, she needed to understand what she'd forgotten. Maybe the memories were gone, but something remained. Otherwise why didn't she come out of the hospital or rehab smiling? Ready to greet each day happy?

Instead she'd come out of it pensive. Not timid but...careful. The way they'd been in Afghanistan on that last tour. Taking an hour to drive down a strip of road that would've taken five minutes in Wisconsin.

Because you never knew what was buried in the road, ready to destroy you and your team. Your buddies. The men who'd become his family.

And when they died...he'd grieved as much as if Jerry lay lifeless on the blood-stained road next to him.

"Are you okay?" She pulled away from him, frowning slightly.

He swallowed and pushed back rage and the roar of pain inside him. He was supposed to comfort her. Instead she was comforting him.

Something grew in him. Affection. And more. He wanted to hold her. To put his cheek against hers. To close his eyes and breathe in her scent.

But that would scare her more. She wasn't ready for that.

"You're ready for it." The thought was insidious. A whisper that didn't seem to come from his mind or his soul but from outside of him.

Not God's voice, though it sounded familiar.

Morrisey. With a bit of the Midwestern, country boy twang.

He shook his head. A hell of a time to hear voices.

"How do you think we feel?" This voice had a different feel. Still a Midwestern twang but with an inner city sneer that the army never knocked out of T. J. *"We're dead. Eight days later and I'd be back in Minnesota. Lousy timing."*

Nia started to pull back. He flattened his hands on her back, feeling her ribs through the thin material of her shirt. With a soft sound halfway between a sob and a laugh, she rested against him, her body loose, not trying to get away anymore. Trusting him. Or maybe she just needed someone to value her.

Wasn't that what everyone needed?

"You still have lousy timing," he said to his phantom buddies. *"Go away."*

Two laughs echoed in his head...and then they shut up. Gone. Leaving him alone. Though of course they'd never been there. It was his own messed-up mind talking. In reality, there was only him and Nia and a few flies.

But inside him, his heart that had been closed down for too long sighed and opened up. Ready to let Nia in.

The hell of it was that she was more damaged than he was.

And he'd only known her for a couple hours.

A closed-up, cautious woman.

And he was a closed-up, cautious man.

Like two metal lockers butting up against each other and no key to unlock them.

It didn't matter. None of it mattered. He thought of a saying he'd heard or read somewhere, something that stuck in his mind because of its stupidity: *The heart knew what the heart knew.*

If that were so, his heart had a hell of a sense of humor.

"None of this is your fault," he said. "You exhibited the classic symptoms of PTSD. The unexplained fits of anger, the depression, the tantrums, the anxiety. The silence."

She lifted her head and he saw damp tear tracks on her face. "Couldn't I have been...a bad kid?"

"No." The word came out with no hesitation. "No," he said again. More firmly this time, though the firmness had been there before. There in his heart.

She was light in his arms, but he didn't hold her lightly. He held her as if she were someone precious.

He'd only known her for hours, but it seemed as if he'd known her forever. In another life. On a soul level.

He'd never believed in that soul crap before.

And he didn't know if he believed in it now.

"Maybe you're just saying this because I'm seducing you," she said.

"Are you?"

She frowned, the marks of the tears still made a path down her pale skin, but the tears had stopped.

It made him fiercely grateful. Made him want to keep this line of conversation going.

"I don't think so," Nia said.

"In that case, maybe I'm seducing you."

God knew he wanted to seduce her. That part of him was still working overtime. Or it would, if he let it.

She laughed and he felt her laughter in his chest, slicing through the darkness that wrapped around him, letting in rays of sunlight.

He smiled but the movement felt stiff. Like a muscle that hadn't been used for a long time. Her laughter slowed, then stopped. She shifted and he loosened his arms.

"Thank you." She twisted off him, onto the cushion. Perched on the edge, she faced him. "I can't remember what happened. And I never will." She cupped her hand over the left side of her head, her slender fingers curved over the top. "I might grow new brain cells, but the ones that stored those memories of my whole life until almost two years ago are destroyed."

He nodded, though he wondered... The actual memories were gone, but he suspected *something* remained in her cells. Some kind of pictureless, wordless memories. Some kind of sense memory.

She *felt*. He knew she felt deeply. That's why as a child, she'd had the easy fall into depression. Into self-destruction. That's why she'd damaged the lives of the people who should've saved her, but instead blamed her.

As far as he knew, she hadn't exhibited any of that behavior since she moved to Miracle. Maybe he was sometimes oblivious as to what was going on around him, but Jerry would've mentioned it. In his way, Jerry was as bad as the two village gossips: Linda Wegner at Wegner's, the village general store, and Angie Schuster at La Curl (We Do Men, Too). With Angie, *do* meant she skewered men with her tongue in a way men didn't want to be skewered with a tongue.

But Jerry was unlike the other two, saving the gossip

just for Rob. There wasn't much Rob missed about Miracle, even when he'd been six thousand miles away in Afghanistan.

The only thing Jerry didn't tell Rob was where he disappeared to three nights a week.

Nia's hand dropped. Rob lifted his and placed it on the side of her head, in the exact spot where her palm had been. Under his fingertips, he felt a slight depression. Instead of jerking back from fear, she leaned into his palm, her eyes wide with trust.

Tenderness grew in him. It filled all his cells. If there were any open spaces in his body, between bones, between blood vessels, the tenderness nudged in and cuddled, saying *I'm good, I'm good. I'm so damn cute and so damn good.*

He imagined Jack's Magic Beanstalk didn't grow faster and wider and more clinging than the cloying tenderness.

The dark, threatening cloud was...gone. As gone as if it had never been an inch near him, much less wrapped around him like skin over bones.

Only the sun remained. Shining inside him.

"Tell me what it was like," he said and heard the hoarseness in his voice, as if he'd been the one soundlessly crying, "when you woke up from the coma."

She sat straight and frowned, her eyes lowered. Looking inward. When she spoke, her voice was soft. Almost as if she talked to herself.

"I just remember seeing a light and hearing a scream in my head. I don't think there were any thoughts. I didn't have words yet. Words had been...knocked out of my mind, so I couldn't think. I just...felt." She stopped. Swallowed. Her gaze still downward. Then her chest lifted.

"Fear," she said, her voice shaky. "That's what I felt. Confusion. Fear. Uncertainty. And more fear. Then there was a voice. Someone talking loudly. Then calling out. Next, people swarmed around me, saying things I didn't understand. Their voices worried."

Her gaze flicked up at him. Silently asking whether she should go on. He nodded.

"The only one who ever asked me besides you was Dr. Whitcomb," she said.

"I'm glad someone cared."

"I think he was curious in a...doctor way." Her eyebrows contracted. "Scientific."

He nodded, not happy with Dr. Whitcomb.

Nia was a person, not a science experiment.

"At first, I didn't even know *what* they were." She gestured from her chest to his. "That they were people and I was a person, too. For all I knew, I could've been a cat. Or a bug. I think I felt closer to a bug with all these giant people hanging over my bed."

She stopped to swallow, and he wanted to say something. But he didn't know what to say yet. He didn't want to stop the flow of words. Or feelings. He knew what that was like, since his feelings were still stuck inside him. A giant barbed-wire ball of feelings.

He couldn't blame anyone at the VA. They'd tried but they couldn't cut through the barbed-wire-protected belief that he should have saved T. J. and Morrisey. Not even his twin could push through the prickly ball. Not even when Rob knew it was irrational.

Only Nia made it past the damn ball. Without even trying, she'd walked through his invisible barrier as if it were never there.

"I think noises started coming out of my mouth," she continued. "Probably nothing that made sense. And then someone gave me a shot. When I came to I was in a different room. The light was dimmer. And someone spoke in a soft voice."

Her eyes closed, her body relaxed, and her face tilted upward as she sorted through her memories. Looking at her, he felt his spirits lift in response, the ball inside him not quite so large and hard and brittle.

At least someone at the damn hospital had some brains. And maybe some heart, to put her in her own room.

"It was a woman." Nia's voice was slow and soft, as if she were talking about a dream she'd had. "I found out later she was one of the nurses. I was scared again but she touched my arm carefully. The way I'd touch a strange cat."

"Like this?" he asked and ran his fingertips along her arm, over her the material of her long-sleeved top.

"Just like that," she whispered, staring at his fingers.

"And then what?" he asked, still skimming his fingertips along her arm.

"She went away, and I started to cry. I don't know why." Nia's voice thickened and the skin around her eyes reddened.

"I think I know." He felt her pain, her confusion, and he ached to make her better. "You were like a newborn. You needed to be held."

She frowned, as if unsure of what he meant.

"Like this." He slid an arm beneath her thighs and curved his other arm around her back. She was light; he lifted her onto his lap with hardly any strain on his muscles. He loosened his arms then, careful to hold her the same way he would cradle a baby or any small animal.

She leaned against him with a long sigh. Only then

did he hold her tightly. Feeling that she needed it. Knowing he needed it as much as her...and maybe more. Because apparently he didn't come alone. He came with passengers.

FOURTEEN

Humans. Debbie talked and talked, like a wind that kept blowing, while Jerry sat on the stiff chair in the small living room and nodded, his eyes glazing over.

Bast watched from her hiding place behind the couch. Debbie's house wasn't much bigger than the apartment where Bast had been imprisoned with the old lady in Milwaukee, though Bast had already ascertained that Debbie's house had an upstairs. When Debbie let Jerry in, Bast had scuttled in after him, her tail up so it wouldn't get caught in the door. Then she'd darted behind the other chair in the corner.

Neither of the humans had spotted her. Not even in the car.

Of course not. They weren't natural born hunters like her. They needed weapons and tools, their hunting instincts dulled.

Jerry snuck a peek toward the back of the house, and Bast had to keep herself from jumping on his lap and giving him a good swat on the top of his head – with her claws extended.

Jerry needed to do more than look. He needed to act.

This was a waste of Bast's nap time.

The sun was shining down on the stuffy room. Instead of curled up on the slanted sunny rectangle on the couch, Bast was hiding in the chair's dark shadow.

She was not happy. Not happy at all.

She craned her head up. Sniffing, she smelled the perfume the other woman had worn today, like strong-smelling flowers. Bast preferred Nia's smell. Nia smelled like Nia. Nothing or no one else smelled like her. Just as no other cat smelled like Bast. It didn't make sense to Bast that so many humans didn't like their natural scent.

But it wasn't her job to figure out why humans did the things they did. It was only her job to help her human.

That wasn't going to happen while she cowered behind the chair.

"I really need to see your cousin," Jerry said. Again. Bast wasn't keeping track of how many times he said that. Keeping track was something humans did. But it was a lot.

Debbie opened her mouth, probably to repeat the same story about Justine sleeping again, but Jerry spoke first. Talking about calling the sheriff. Again. Probably by now Debbie knew he wasn't going to do that anymore than he'd cough up a hairball.

If Bast listened to this one more time, she might cough up a hairball.

Her mind made up, she darted forward and raced across the room.

In her peripheral vision, Jerry jumped off the chair onto his feet. "What the hell—"

Debbie shrieked. "A cat! There's a cat in my house."

Bast didn't stop. In the hall, she saw a kitchen across from the living room. To her left was a bathroom and probably another bedroom. On her right was a stairway covered with green carpet. Bast could smell the overly sweet flower scent that Justine had worn, leading up the steps. She may as well have left a trail of tuna crumbs.

"Come back here!" Debbie called, her voice screechy.

"Jerry, you can't do that."

Bast bounded up the steps, not afraid to make noise. Not caring that Nia said she sounded like a runaway horse when she pounded up the steps.

A horse should be proud to make noise like her.

A horse would be proud to be anything like her.

No human rode her. With cats, it was the other way around. Once in a while, Bast allowed Nia to carry her a few steps before she jumped off.

"You can't go upstairs without a search warrant," Debbie shouted as Bast reached the landing. On one side was a bedroom with one wall slanted. On the other was a small bathroom.

"I'm catching the cat," Jerry said, still in the hall when, in Bast's opinion, he should've shoved Debbie aside and followed Bast up the stairs. "Why, what do you have to hide?"

"Nothing."

"Then you won't mind if I go upstairs."

A man's boot stomped onto the first step as Bast followed the smell into the bedroom and saw a lump on the bed that looked like a log covered with a blanket. Bast couldn't hear any breathing, but that was probably because her heart was thundering from the dash upstairs.

Aiming for the bed, she took a flying leap that gave her five-pound body the landing power of a fifty-pound dog. She slammed down with a loud thump that should've woken Justine. Instead, Nia's sister lay there, as still as a broken doll, breathing so shallowly that her chest didn't move.

Jerry thudded into the room, his breath harsh.

From the stairway came plodding steps and huffing breaths.

Ignoring the extraneous noises, Bast stepped up to the woman's face, curved her neck down, and pushed her nose up to Justine's parted lips.

A warm puff of air breathed out. So small it was like a kitten's breath instead of a grown human's.

This was how her lady in Milwaukee was at the end. Her breaths getting smaller and smaller until they disappeared.

Bast had waited and waited, but her breaths never came back.

"What the hell are you doing?" Jerry yelled, rushing to the bed.

Bast hissed and leapt onto the dresser tucked into the corner of the room. Poised to leap away if he came near her, she watched while he bent over the sleeping woman. Just like Bast had done, though he inspected her with his eyes and not his nose. Lines pleated his forehead.

As he pressed two fingers against the woman's neck, Debbie burst into the room, huffing louder than an old, large dog in the summer heat.

"Get away," Debbie said between gasps. "She's sleeping."

He whipped out his cell phone and she screeched. "No! Don't call anyone!"

He turned his head and Bast watched as Debbie jumped at him. Moving swiftly for a woman who wheezed, she knocked the phone out of his hand.

"You're fucking crazy." Jerry glared at her, his anger vibrating in the small room, tension bouncing off the walls. "Something is wrong with her. She needs help."

"She doesn't need anything." Her voice high and thin, Debbie exuded fear, the scent powerful. "She's fine. Honest. I only gave her a small pill to relax her."

He stiffened, his gaze on her sharpening. "You gave

her a pill? With or without her permission?"

Debbie's gaze slid away from his. "It's just a sedative. A small one. It's not even that strong."

"Could be she's allergic."

"No! I know she's taken it before. She told me."

"She did, huh? When did this discussion take place?" He stooped and felt for the phone on the floor, not taking his gaze off Debbie.

Bast thought that was the first smart move he'd made since he came into the house.

An even smarter move would be to walk out of here and pretend he never saw Justine like this. To let her die.

But Bast could see he didn't trust Debbie.

He wasn't as dumb as a dog after all.

"On the drive back from Miriam's house," Debbie's voice quavered, sounding old, "Justine was talking crazy. I didn't know what she might do. I just wanted to calm her down a little."

"So you gave her the little pill."

"Just a Xanex. I know Justine's not allergic. She said she'd used it before and had just recently quit."

"She agreed to take it?"

Bast didn't understand everything they talked about, but she understood that Debbie gave Justine a food that made her sick. Bast had eaten plants that made her sick. She puked and then was better.

It was obvious what they needed to do: make Justine puke.

Humans made everything hard.

"Yes. That's what happened." Debbie nodded vigorously, and another dog image popping up in Bast's mind, a shaggy, overeager dog with flapping skin. One that was thinking: *Like me, like me.* And even louder: *Feed me, feed me.*

Cats sometimes groomed themselves with vigor. They sometimes ate with vigor. Bast had pounced on a mouse with vigor. But she never agreed with anything a human said so vigorously. Not even for food.

She had her standards.

"Debbie, she didn't really say yes, did she?" Jerry's voice was like Bast's before she was ready to strike out with her claws. Smooth and deadly. Nothing doglike about it.

"I just wanted to calm her down." Debbie's lips turned upside-down. "Really, it's all her fault. If she was allergic, she should've told me."

Jerry turned and walked across to the other side of the dresser from Bast. Hissing, Bast backed up against the wall. He gave her a sideways look, then picked up a bottle and then another. When he turned, he was holding the second bottle in his hand. He brought it to Debbie.

"Xanex." Her mouth opened and closed twice. "She *lied* to me."

"Yeah, well, sue her." He set it on the dresser. "More likely, if she lives, she'll sue you."

"She was talking crazy. I was afraid she'd go back and kill Nia." Debbie opened her eyes wide. "I was saving Nia's life."

"Yeah, right." He put the cell phone to his mouth. "The village should give you an award."

Debbie stared at him and her lower lip trembled. She crossed her arms and this time didn't try to stop him.

When he put the phone in his jacket pocket, she said in a voice that wheezed out of her throat, "What are you going to do to me?"

"What do you think I should do?"

"She threatened to kill her sister. I had to do *something*. One sister's not right in the head, and this one's crazy, too."

Jerry smiled but his eyes narrowed. "Looks like crazy runs in her family."

Debbie's eyes blazed at him. The hair on Bast's spine stood straight up and her nails drew out.

Bast thought about scratching Debbie's eyes out. She'd never done it to a human yet, though she'd left a scar on a man's face.

He would think twice about kicking the next cat.

This one... Bast had seen the way Debbie looked at Nia, had sensed her confused emotions. Hatred and jealousy...and hurt and fear. Too many emotions for a human. They couldn't handle it.

They all needed more naps.

But if Debbie hurt Nia, all the naps in the world wouldn't save Debbie. Bast would find her and hurt her a thousand times more.

"Do you want to see me beg?" Debbie's voice cracked and she bent forward, put her hands on the mattress, then got down on her knees, her movements clumsy even for a human. Finally, she knelt on the floor and gazed up at Jerry.

Bast had to stop herself from hissing to show her opinion of a human on her knees in front of another. It disgusted her. If she weren't hiding, she would throw up her breakfast. Some humans had no self-respect.

"I'll do it, if that's what you want," Debbie said. "Please don't tell them I gave Justine the Xanex. I swear I just did it to calm her. I didn't plan this." She swept her hand toward the woman conked out on the bed.

From the highway, the thin wail of a siren came to Bast's ears. Too far away for the humans to hear.

"All I have is this house," Debbie said, and her voice wobbled. "Nothing else. Justine would take it if she could. She's greedy like that. But I would never hurt her. Not on purpose."

"What about Nia? You'd hurt her, wouldn't you?"

She shook her head vigorously, then splayed her hand on the carpet to push herself up in a way that looked painful to Bast, like an old lady. Made harder because of Debbie's extra weight.

"I promise I'll never hurt her." She put her hand to her heart. "If you want me to, I'll swear on a Bible."

In the silence that followed, Jerry tipped his head toward the highway, and Bast could see he heard the siren.

"You keep that promise," he said, "and I'll leave you alone."

She brightened. "Thank you! Thank you, thank you, thank you." Her hands held out, she took a step toward Jerry. "You're so generous. So warm. You have a good heart. I'm so grateful to you."

"Don't be." He held out his arms to stave her off.

Then the sirens wails came closer, near enough for even Debbie to hear. She gasped and turned in the direction of the driveway.

Bast narrowed her eyes at Jerry. She knew what the ambulance meant. Someone was going to take Justine to a place where they would give her shots, then lock her in a cage where they would keep her until she was better and could go home. Like the place Bast had gone to when she was younger. Only this was a place for people.

Why did he do that? First he was letting Debbie go, and now saving Justine.

He should let Justine die.

Justine smelled...wrong. Evil. Every cat knew what to do when they spotted an evil creature sniffing around their home...

First they caught them.

Then they killed them.

And after that, they ate them.

Debbie turned her head. "The ambulance is there. Justine will be all right. Look," She leaned over Justine and patted her limp hand. "Still breathing. Even two Xanex shouldn't harm her."

"You don't know if it's only two," Jerry said. "She lied about taking the drug. And you know who lies?"

Frowning slightly, Debbie shook her head. A fearful look on her face said she didn't want to know.

"Addicts," Jerry said. "You can't trust anything they say."

Debbie's forehead wrinkled. "I guess you'd know. With your dad and all."

The siren grew louder, stopping on the street in front of the house. Debbie peered out the window and missed the look Jerry sent her. As if he'd like to put his hands on her back and shove her out the window.

Bast saw it. Bast saw all the important things.

"Thank God everyone is talking about Pastor Jim cheating on Becky," Debbie said. "We might just miss being the center of gossip."

Jerry looked at her as if she were spoiled food that was beginning to attract flies and vultures. Bast had the same feeling.

It was time to leave.

Bast leapt off the dresser, then padded down the stairs. In the hall, she crouched against the wall near the front door. When the ambulance people came into the house to get Justine, she would race outside.

She didn't know if Jerry was going to the hospital or not, but it didn't matter. She would find her way home by herself.

This way, if something happened to Nia later on and if Bast thought there was a tiny chance that Debbie might be involved, she would find her way back without any problem...and make Debbie pay.

FIFTEEN

Everything happened too fast for Nia. As if she'd stepped onto an escalator and discovered it was a jet plane. Her phone call to Dr. Whitcomb's office started as usual when she was put on hold right away. She told Rob that Dr. Whitcomb's receptionist would make her wait a few minutes, then tell her the doctor would call her back. When he did call her back, he'd tell her he would discuss it at their next appointment, which was down to once a month now.

She suspected he wanted to see her more, but that's all the insurance company would pay and he wasn't going to talk to her for free.

But this time, instead of the receptionist returning, Dr. Whitcomb came on the phone, his voice ponderous. It took Nia a second to adjust her mind to the shock. She would have felt less surprised to hear God – and she wasn't sure if God existed.

She supposed most people would be more surprised to hear a cat speak than God.

And most of them wouldn't be surprised at all to hear Dr. Whitcomb's monotone voice tell her she should come right away.

Not her. She didn't expect anything. Sometimes she felt as if the only thing she could expect was that Bast would allow Nia to take care of her.

But now Rob seemed to want to stay with her and

protect her. She didn't understand what happened there.

And Dr. Whitcomb was treating her as if it mattered to him that someone had been at her doorstep with a gun in her purse...

Two minutes later, she was getting into Rob's car, holding tight to her purse and her whirling thoughts.

"This isn't normal," she said as they drove out of the village, the highway speed changing from thirty-five miles per hour to fifty-five. Leaving behind them 628 residents, uncounted dogs and cats, and who knew how many rabbits, squirrels, birds, and other creatures.

"What isn't normal?" The car stereo was on low, playing "Unchained Melody" by the Righteous Brothers.

Nia felt a little unchained herself. She'd awoken this morning expecting another day of observation and learning how to act like a normal, functioning person.

She hadn't expected this much learning. It was like expecting a scoopful of ice cream and getting a gallon. Way too much to digest. Only instead of a stomachache, it was making her dizzy.

That's when she remembered...

"You know about the miracle, right?" she asked.

"The prophecy? Yeah." He glanced at her. "You don't believe that, do you?"

On the stereo, two men sang in beautiful harmony that time was going by slowly.

They were wrong. Time was speeding by. So fast it was stealing her breath.

"I saw it," she said. "Just before the church people swarmed out." Like ants smelling picnic food, she thought, picturing it in her mind. It happened a week ago from last Sunday. Eight days past. The row of cars with one perfect letter on each dirty rear window, with a car unmarked between the words to show a space. Spelling out A MIRACLE IS COMING.

Thinking about it, goose bumps formed troops and marched along her arms.

"I don't go to church," Rob said. "You see who did it?"

She rubbed her forearms. "I was there, and I don't know. I walked past the church that morning to go to the store for cat food." She rested her hands on her lap. "There were no letters on any of the cars. I came back ten minutes later, and the letters were on the windows. That's when the doors opened and people swarmed out."

"There was no one else there before that?"

"No one. And no paint on any of the windows. I would've noticed."

His face darkened. "And then the commotion started."

She nodded. The excited voices, and frightened ones. A few angry, looking to see if anyone was playing tricks. Looking at her.

Her skin had broken into sweat and she left, not wanting to get dragged into it. Like being in the eye of a hurricane. "I didn't see anyone until then."

"Pastor Jim seemed to think it was kids with lasers."

"In that case, they were very fast kids."

He took his eyes off the highway to glance at her sharply. "You believe in God?"

"I've never seen God." Unless God was a talking cat.

Or an invisible force that wrote messages on car windows.

Maybe that was God's way of talking to her.

Maybe the prophecy was meant for her.

After all, she was the first to see it.

But wouldn't it have been easier for God to just appear and talk to her? In her living room, maybe? She'd let God sit on the comfortable chair. She'd take the uncomfortable one. Or sit on the floor. After all, she sat on the floor while her cat curled up on the couch and peered at her, face to face.

Angels. She'd read about angels. Maybe angels did it.

"You think your psychiatrist being available and telling you to come on in counts as a miracle?"

"No. But Dr. Whitcomb saying he'll make sure the insurance pays for it might be a miracle."

He laughed, a spontaneous happy sound. And for an instant, the sky brightened. Or maybe *she* brightened.

Or maybe it was the miracle happening.

"You're the miracle," she said.

His laughter abruptly shut off. "I'm no one's miracle."

They drove in silence for another forty minutes until they reached the clinic. Five minutes later, she was in the doctor's office, sitting on one black chair with arms and Rob was seated on another one, a small table between them. Across from them, Dr. Whitcomb sat in his chair that had a tufted, recliner back.

Neither Nia's chair nor Rob's reclined, but she had no inclination to sit back, so it never bothered her. Especially not today, with her mind doing an imitation of a grasshopper, jumping from thought to thought. Next to her, Rob told Dr. Whitcomb about her suspicions of an intruder, her sister's visit, then his belief that Nia had been abused as a child.

Rob spoke in short sentences, a hard edge to his voice as Dr. Whitcomb looked at him through his rimless glasses with complete concentration, leaning forward more than usual. When Rob finished, Dr. Whitcomb sat back and adjusted his glasses, the way he always did before he proclaimed something important.

Nia clenched her hands in her lap and waited.

"I suspected she might have PTSD," Dr. Whitcomb

said, his roundish face with jolly Santa Claus cheeks not looking particularly jolly today. Or any day, really. His demeanor giving the message that life was a serious business.

"You never said anything." Nia leaned forward to remind him this was about her, not Rob.

"It's not for me to say," he said, his voice neutral.

"The hell it isn't." The words rang out of Rob, nothing neutral about them. "PTSD isn't something that should be ignored."

"Normally I wouldn't, but Nia's case is different." Dr. Whitcomb turned back to Nia and gave her a smile that was almost gentle and caring, but it looked off, and she wondered if he practiced it in the mirror to give the impression that he cared. "I didn't make the decision not to tell you. That was Dr. Ormand."

She looked at Rob. "Dr. Whitcomb's only been my psychiatrist for two months here. Dr. Ormand was my psychiatrist in Minnesota after I came out of the coma."

"How long were you in the coma?" Rob asked.

"Three months. I was in rehab for eighteen months. They were looking for a place to put me when I found out I inherited my great-aunt's house."

He nodded and looked back at Dr. Whitcomb. "Did Ormand tell the police about the PTSD?"

"Oh no." Dr. Whitcomb's eyes widened slightly though he kept his voice even. "The letters show no proof that any abuse happened. The police would never have arrested anyone on a supposition. Besides, there was nothing to show any connection to the accident."

Rob's hand on the chair of his arm curled into a fist. "How often have you seen Nia since she became your patient?"

Dr. Whitcomb frowned and didn't answer right away.

"Four times," Nia said promptly, "counting today."

"In the previous three times, you could've told her."

"I agreed with Dr. Ormand." Dr. Whitcomb patted a file on the table next to his recliner chair. As if it held all her secrets. "I didn't see a need for her to know."

"Why?" she asked. Bringing his attention back to her. And it felt like the cry came from deep in her belly. A *why* about everything.

Rob was right to come here. She wasn't sure if she *wanted* to know her past. But to get better – to get past it – she needed to know.

"You were like Sleeping Beauty." Dr. Whitcomb leaned forward and a spark lit in both his eyes, his Santa Claus cheeks turning pink with excitement. "Waking up with no memory, no emotional damage, no fears."

"No fears." She heard the harshness in her voice. "I was *filled* with fears."

"Not that kind." He leaned back, his expression neutral again, as if he recalled he was talking to his patient and not another professional. Someone who might have a more personal take on the situation.

As she stared at him, it occurred to her that she was the chicken about to be roasted. And Dr. Whitman was the chef sharpening his knives.

"The fears you had after you came out of the coma were normal fears of the unknown. But what happened to you before the accident..." He gestured with both of his palms up. "As an army veteran, Mr. Ackerman can tell you that it's small stuff compared to the trauma he's talking about."

"It's not small stuff to her," Rob said.

Dr. Whitcomb's left eyebrow rose. "Do you really think her blank mind is worse than memories of abuse? Either physical or emotional? Ongoing since she was a child? Something that made her alienate and exploit others in return?" He gestured at Nia, who once again had the feeling she was a spectator to this discussion about her life. Like watching a movie in which people talked and talked but she didn't believe it, because they didn't care.

Her hands clenched. She cared. She cared enough to do something crazy.

"Look at her now. Her comparative calmness and acceptance. Why, she's almost normal."

"Bullshit. She's not living life. She's walking around in a vacuum."

Nia turned to him, her spine stiff. He didn't notice, his scowling attention on Dr. Whitcomb.

Didn't Rob realize he was doing the same thing? Not living life? From what she understood, he lived in his brother's house most of the time like a hermit.

Wasn't that walking around in a vacuum?

Except today.

Her hands unclenched and her fingers separated. The stiffness eased from her body, her tight muscles loosening.

Today had been different for her. Rob had held her in his arms. She'd cried in his arms. Today she'd gotten close to another person.

Until today, the only living being she could recall feeling close to was Bast.

"We've been over this before," Dr. Whitcomb said. "Again, it wasn't my decision, but what difference would it have made if she'd known that abuse was a possibility? It would have added an extra...sadness." Dr. Whitcomb sat straight in his chair, his posture defensive. "In any case, nothing in her files supports this accusation. It's only speculation. If you're talking about the attack on her that caused the brain damage, the vehicle that ran over her, that could have been anyone. It might have been a stranger who'd never seen her before. Someone with his or her own emotional problems. It's possible she was at the wrong place at the wrong time."

"A random attack?" Rob's words shot out of his mouth like bullets. "Someone tried to *kill* her. She was run over twice, then left for dead. That sounds personal to me."

Nia's muscles stiffened again. Her throat closed.

She told herself to keep calm. That she was just an observer.

But that wasn't working for her today.

She wasn't a witness to her life. She was at the center of it. Living it.

"And what about the hate letters from the family?" Rob's face darkened, and she could see he spoke through his teeth. "She has four letters, four suspects. The only member of her family that didn't write a hate letter was her brother."

"I've explained Dr. Ormand's position," Dr. Whitcomb said, his voice as unyielding as his posture, "which coincides with my own. If you feel so strongly, *you* should take it up with the police."

Rob looked at her. "Did the police say anything to you about your family members?"

She shook her head and felt something stir inside her. Something twisty and uncomfortable. Something that had been hiding inside her all along, like a sleeping bear.

And the bear was waking now. And the bear had a name.

Fear.

"Reading the letters from your family," Rob continued, "did you suspect they might have tried to kill you?"

Once again, she shook her head. Even as the fear grew in her belly, heavy and dark and bristly.

She was lying again. Of course, she suspected. But she pushed it down like she did everything with emotion.

It was too unsettling to delve into. She would much rather concentrate on the day-to-day part of life. Much rather concentrate on the people who lived in Miracle. Watching their lives and interactions as she talked about it to Bast, who listened to her so carefully. When Bast was awake, of course. Nia understood that cats needed their naps.

Perhaps that's what her mind was doing this last year and a half. A human kind of awake-sleep.

"I don't know where you're going with this." Dr. Whitcomb slid forward to the edge of the chair, the soles of his black leather shoes flat on the short-napped gray carpet. "Now that Nia knows PTSD is a possibility, I'll be happy to incorporate that into our sessions. But any assumptions on your part or even mine are just suppositions. None of it would stand up in court."

"We're not in court." Rob stood, his legs braced. "She's your *patient*. You should be concerned about treating her emotional health."

"You're getting angry." Dr. Whitcomb stood. "Would it be safe to say that you've had experience with PTSD?"

"You don't get it. This isn't about you or me. Someone tried to kill her, and it could happen again."

Nia stood. The air was thick with anger and tension. She didn't like this feeling. Not at all.

Dr. Whitcomb stood, too. "Mr. Ackerman, if anyone is upsetting Nia, it's you. Can't you see what you're doing to her?"

Rob looked at her sharply. And the tightness of anger

changed. His lips formed a grimace. His eyebrows contracted.

"Nia?" he asked.

She stepped toward him and held out her hand. "Let's go."

He gazed into her eyes as if trying to see through them, all the way into her soul.

The hot, prickly ball inside her shrunk. She took another step toward him.

"Nia!" Dr. Whitcomb's voice was sharp. "We should make another appointment about this. You need to talk to me. You need my help."

She turned her head slightly. "You don't tell me the truth."

"I don't know the truth. No one knows."

"You know." She stared at him for another moment, and his eye skittered away from hers. She turned her gaze back to Rob. "Let's split this joint," she said.

He laughed, and his eyes lit up brilliantly.

Inside her the tension eased and the anger cooled. As they walked out of the office, Rob took her hand. Her breath stopped but she kept her head up and her step never faltered. Hand in hand, they closed the door behind them.

Gone from Dr. Whitcomb's office.

Off to search for the truth.

And inside Nia, the bear rumbled...

SIXTEEN

Rob stood slightly behind Nia at her right and watched her handle the computer as if she'd been born plugged into one, perhaps with an umbilical cord that came with a USB plug.

A good fit for her. Computers were easier to deal with than people and emotions. He understood that. Especially with the black cloud of grief he'd been trying to ignore for so long that kept lowering. Threatening to suffocate him and drown him in darkness.

He shoved it away from him. Roaring in his head at the damn thing.

The cloud came back. Thicker. Darker. Not alone. Bringing with it the bloody images of Morrisey and T. J.

Not now, he shouted in his mind. *I can't take care of you now. I have to watch her. Save her.*

Morrisey on his right moved first, his lips lifting to form a macabre half-smile. A dead man's smile.

Not like his eyes. They sparked. Fully alive.

A whisper came from his left. A thread of a sound. He turned, though he knew there was only a wall with a picture of a ballerina. But instead of the rail-thin woman with an ivory face, he saw the white grin of his dark-skinned friend who'd been a brother to him. A brother of his heart if not his blood.

A dead brother.

"Go get her, bro," T. J. said.

"Time to start living again." Morrisey's husky voice caught his attention, and he turned to his right. But Morrisey's half blown-off face was already fading. Just a cut-off smile left. Like a damaged, mostly human Cheshire cat.

Above Rob the cloud dispersed, leaving him sweating and struggling for breath.

Nia swiveled in her chair to look at him, her creased forehead showing her concern.

He shook his head, his teeth clenched to keep them from chattering. When he stepped back, her forehead smoothed and her lips tightened. She turned back to the computer, her shoulders hunched. Protecting herself. As if waiting for a blow.

He closed his eyes for a long moment, his breath still shuddering. His whole body shuddering.

He couldn't tell her.

But if he didn't, she would never know.

And didn't she deserve to know the truth from someone?

"It's me." He heard his voice croak, as if it were a rusted gate.

She glanced over her right shoulder that was still hunched. Frowning, she didn't say anything.

He couldn't blame her. She was probably thinking the cat was more open. She'd be right. Maybe he should tell the cat and then ask the cat to tell her. Bast seemed to have better communication skills than him.

"I'm alive," he said.

She continued to stare at him. But her shoulder relaxed and lowered. Not all the way but at least a good inch.

Okay, that wasn't exactly an explanation. Or as his mother would say, *"I don't know what the heck you're talking about."*

Nia's head tilted, watching him sideways out of her gray-green eyes. "Afghanistan?"

He nodded.

"That's why you know so much about PTSD?"

He nodded again.

He should say more, but what? That he woke up sweating and calling out names of ghosts? That his brother cried over him? That thunder made him put on his iPod headphones and slam the music up loud?

And worse... Should he tell her he'd failed Morrisey and T. J. in the worst way possible? That he didn't know why the hell he was alive...and they weren't?

He clamped his jaws so tight his gums hurt. He should've died with them. Died with the others.

She swiveled back to the computer, and he didn't blame her. He couldn't explain the way he felt to her. He couldn't explain it to the doctors. They would talk about survivor's guilt. As if that knowledge put it into a nice packet. And, hey, here's a pill that will make you walk around like a zombie. And when that doesn't work, you start to think that maybe you should take more than what was prescribed. Maybe you should take the whole bottle.

A breath shuddered out of him. He put his hand on her shoulder and she flinched.

He jerked back. He deserved that rebuff.

But he would make it up to her. He was human. He made mistakes. Next time the ghosts came, he would manage them better.

"I'm sorry," he said.

She swiveled and half smiled, half nodded at him, then turned back to the computer.

In that small, half moment of time, the room

brightened. The air lightened. The cloud lifted.

He drew in a deep breath and glanced around. Once again okay for now. Free from an attack of guilt. Free from the cloud.

He forced himself to pay attention to the office. The only modern things in it were the computer desk, the computer equipment, and Nia. The cream-colored walls had a yellowish patina. Paintings of ballet dancers hung on the wall. Rob guessed they'd been there when Nia had moved in and she'd left them up.

Their almost painfully thin bodies reminded him of Nia.

He'd known her for barely hours, but he suspected from now on almost everything he saw would remind him of her. Even if they were nothing like her, their difference would make him think of her.

His fingers twitched with another urge to draw her. Right now. To catch the curve of her long neck as she typed and the play of sunlight and shadow dancing on her skin.

The slight curve of her breasts beneath the purple-blue shirt.

Her breasts without the purple-blue shirt...

"Don't you want to see?" she asked.

SEVENTEEN

He started and realized she was staring at him with two puzzled lines between her eyebrows. That she really wasn't reading his mind and didn't know what he wanted to see.

"Ah, sure. You're good at this."

She patted the chair next to him, one with a vinyl seat that reminded him of chairs in the principal's room when he was a kid. "Sit and learn."

He sat on the chair and glided closer, appreciating the way the chair wheeled. He paid attention to her expression. The haunted look she'd had in the doc's office was still there, but lighter. Just a small haunting now.

"Dr. Whitcomb said I'm good at computers because I'm not afraid of them."

"At his office, he said you were afraid."

"Afraid isn't really the right word. I'm not...comfortable around people. People are..."

"Scary?"

"Strange. They're like puzzles I can't figure out."

"I'm strange."

She gave him a smile that carried a lot of sad in it. "You're like me. Damaged."

Something swelled in him. Something that made him feel that maybe someday he could be...happy

It took him a second to recognize the emotion.

Hope.

His skin prickled with sweat, his heart beat fast again. In an odd way, hope was as scary as hopelessness.

Because he could be wrong.

He wanted to reach out and touch the side of her face like a lover would.

Instead, he curled his fingers at his side.

He was like an inactive volcano coming to life. The lava stirring within, boiling and rumbling. Not erupting yet. But soon. Very soon.

When that happened, there could be destruction.

She turned to the computer. "This is my mother." She angled the laptop so he could see the screen. A woman with dark blond hair and smiling eyes sat at a round table with men in suits and women in evening gowns. There were similar tables around them.

He pushed down his jangled emotions to focus on the image on the screen. He couldn't fix himself, but maybe he could help Nia.

The woman looked like a mature version of Justine, but with a softer edge. He leaned closer, his arm brushing Nia's shoulder. Even sitting, her mother looked tall. Rob caught a bit of Nia in the mother's face. Maybe the shape of her eyes. Doe-eyed with thick lashes.

He scanned the bottom print of the picture from a Minneapolis e-magazine that was covering a fundraising for a children's hospital. It appeared to be honoring the intense, thin man who it described as one of the top cardiac doctor in the United States. The names of the others at the table were mentioned in order, and Nia's mother was the last one named: Brenda Beaudine.

"And this one." Another photo at a hospital event, this one more recent. The mother still had the same color hair, but there was a slight change in her face. Still lovely but more mature. The thin man's dark hair was streaked with gray and the lines that bracketed his lips were deeper.

Nia was already typing in another link, her fingers flying. The image changed. In this one the thin man was standing, and Brenda was gazing up at him, applauding and smiling. They both appeared to be much younger. Brenda looked to be in her twenties. A freshness about the mother's face reminded him of Nia. But it could have been the way the camera caught her. As if she glowed from within.

"She looks happy," Nia said, her voice wistful.

He nodded, feeling grim inside.

"She looks like she's in love," he said.

Her hands froze above the keys. The pads of her fingertips lightly touching them. Her lips were parted when she turned to him, her eyes wary.

"My father isn't in the picture," she said. "Maybe she's thinking about him."

"Maybe she's thinking about going home to her family," he said. "Or getting home and taking off her shoes."

"Or dessert," she said.

He laughed and she looked at him surprised. As if she hadn't realized she said something funny. Then she smiled, and he wanted to lean forward and kiss her, which was a bad idea. Very bad. But it was planted in his brain already, along with more things he wanted to do.

After all, he was a man. The kind that was attracted to women. Not that there was anything wrong with those that didn't. It was a genetic thing, and he had landed firmly in the ballpark of the team that liked to touch and kiss and make love to a woman.

And not just any woman.

Right now it was one specific woman who looked like she could use a good meal, a good haircut, and some very good loving.

Her hair needed to grow before doing anything about the second. But he was willing to take care of the first and third any time. Any time at all.

Creases indented her forehead and she faced the screen again. She pressed the back arrow at the top left, making Rob wish it would be that easy to turn back time. He'd wish a lot of things turned back, undone.

But if they were undone, he and Nia might not be sitting here. He and she might never have met.

She typed in another link. As if she knew it by heart. By a very sad heart.

He tightened his lips. A new picture popped up of her mother and the doctor and he guessed other members of the doctor's staff.

Maybe he was wrong – it wouldn't be the first time, according to his mom and certainly his brother – but he could feel Nia's yearning as she stared at her mother's image.

Though Nia had no memories of her family, he suspected she felt like a bird kicked out of the nest.

"Do you have pictures of your father?" he asked.

She glanced at him, her expression blank. The way she looked when he'd first seen her. Just a few hours ago, though it was hard to believe. Each moment with her was intense. Each second mattered.

Instead of answering, she turned back to the laptop and her fingers danced on the keyboard again. A home page for the Clark Beaudine Realty popped up. A map showed the Minneapolis-St. Paul and Western Wisconsin areas. Before he could look closer, she pressed a link and a picture of a man and a woman came up, both holding up one side of a SOLD sign and smiling widely.

He recognized the woman right away. Justine. Airbrushed, though she didn't need it. He admitted that she was gorgeous – at least on the outside.

Clark Beaudine wouldn't scare buyers away, either. Especially not the women, Rob thought. Not with his golden brown hair that only receded slightly and his white, flashing smile. He was tall and husky. Not fat but the kind of guy who could be fat if he didn't watch what he ate.

His jaw was fleshy, with the beginning of a jowl. Justine's was squarish like his but not yet jowlish. His hair color was the same as Justine's, but the mother's was similar, too. The parents were at the age when gray must be creeping in, and Rob couldn't guess whether their hair color was original.

"What about your brother?" he asked.

"Marc's a contractor in Eau Claire. He works from referrals. I haven't found any pictures of him on the Internet, but I'll try again." She paused, and when she spoke again, there was a note of pride in her voice. "Maybe one of his clients put a picture up. The people on Angie's List give him high ratings."

"Is he much older than you?"

"Two years." She typed in his name for a search. "One woman said her husband left her and didn't pay the bills. Marc finished the job and told her she could pay when she got the money." Her voice thickened. "Another client said his wife had a heart attack. He was in another state on business. Marc went to the hospital and stayed with the wife until their son made it there late that night." Her voice grew smaller. Almost a whisper. "I think he must be a wonderful man."

Rob clenched his jaws to keep from saying that if he

were wonderful, he would've been at his sister's side. He would've come to see her at least once in the hospital.

The first notes of "Real Good Man" filled the air, and he pulled his cell phone out. "Jerry," he said and heard the harshness of his voice.

Nia turned her head away and while Rob listened to his brother, she bent closer to the screen to read the links.

Rob said a few words to Jerry, then shut off his phone and put his hand on her arm.

"Your sister is in the hospital. She had convulsions in the ER and heart palpitations. The doctors want to give her a few tests and keep an eye on her."

EIGHTEEN

"What do you want to do?" Rob asked her.

She looked out the window of Fabrini's, the only Italian restaurant in Miracle. The only restaurant, really, unless she counted the Amber Waves of Grain, which served bar food. Nia had walked in there once last March at dinner time. Men with winter jackets had stopped drinking beer to look at her. She'd turned around and walked out.

Sipping water now, watching cars cruise along the highway that ran through the village, she suspected if she'd been herself before she was run over, she might not have left the bar. If what her sister said was true, she might have enjoyed the attention of the men.

Until now, she wouldn't have believed it. But she shifted her gaze to Rob's austere face and saw the way he looked at her – as if he cared – and the coldness inside her warmed like butter left out in the sun.

She felt like the butter, too. All liquid, all warm. She wanted to bask in that look. She could easily get addicted to it.

"If this were on TV," she said, her voice unusually thick, "I would be at the hospital right now, not sitting here having dinner."

"Is that what you want to do?"

His question made her melt a little more. He was *asking* her, not telling her. She liked that. That was much more sexy than the way the men in the bar had looked at her last March.

But now she had to answer his question. She scratched her forehead. Her ear. The side of her nose.

When she thought about her brother – who she didn't even know – sitting with a woman who didn't mean anything to him, but not coming to visit her in the hospital, she felt...bereaved.

But now she understood why he stayed away. Her sister hadn't been nice to her, and now it was payback.

According to all the letters, Nia hadn't been nice to any of her siblings. Because of that, she didn't blame Marc for not coming.

At least he hadn't written her a nasty letter. She should thank him for that. She was closest in age to him, and must have been with him more than the others. Must have hurt him more.

Then another thought hit her. Like a fist to her belly.

If she'd been suffering from PTSD – if she'd been abused – maybe Marc was, too.

Oh no. Oh no.

She didn't know why it distressed her, as if someone socked her in the middle of her chest, but it did. After all, she couldn't remember what happened. She was sure he remembered. It had to have been worse for him.

Maybe Justine was abused, too. Maybe that's why she turned out so mean.

Or maybe this new theory was wrong. Maybe, if Rob's theory was right, it was just Nia who was abused. Maybe her abuser was a babysitter. Or a teacher. Or a relative.

Or maybe none of this happened. Maybe she was just one of those kids born mean.

She put her hands in her lap to keep from banging her fists on the table. Or putting them to her head and pulling out her hair.

If only she remembered. If only her memory could magically come back.

Magical wasn't the right word.

Miracle. That was the right word.

Or maybe the right word was *disaster.*

Even if an angel or a genie in a bottle – that she pictured looking like Bast – could grant her any wish, she wouldn't ask for those memories. Maybe the real miracle was that the memories were gone. She was starting life over like a house with a makeover.

Some houses were made over to look just like the old one when it was new.

Others were made over completely.

She'd be the made over completely version.

"What's wrong?" Rob asked, and she shook her head. "Just silly things."

A small smile lifted the corners of his lips. "I don't think you could be silly."

Maybe not the old her. But the new, made-over version... She shrugged. This new made-over version might like to be silly.

When this was over, she would add silly to her list. After all, *silly* wasn't too far off from *odd*.

"I don't think Justine wants me at the hospital."

"I don't care what she wants. I only care about you."

Her heart stuttered, then beat steadily again. She shook her head and looked at his lips. And in that second she didn't care if her sister wanted to run out of the hospital wearing only her hospital gown flapping open in the rear, with her backside showing for everyone to see.

She only cared about the man in front of her with brown eyes darkened with concern.

Her gaze lowered to his lips. They looked

soft...kissable.

She wondered what they would feel like. And what he would say if she told him she would like to kiss him.

In the eighteen months since she had woken up in the hospital with the silent scream in her head, she hadn't kissed anyone. Except Bast, of course.

"No," she said, her voice emphatic this time, "I don't want to see her. She doesn't like me and I don't like her."

He smiled at her and she beamed back at him. It felt good to say that. She'd taken a step forward in her life, making a decision instead of sitting in a corner waiting for it all to come together.

"What do you want to do?" he asked.

She didn't want to do anything. But she glanced around, giving herself time to think about his question. The restaurant had been open for only ten minutes when they walked in. Only one other couple was there, a middle-aged man and woman who leaned across the table to murmur to each other. From the speakers came the full, rich voice of a tenor singing opera, the music dramatic and wondrous, and Nia put it on her mental list of things she liked.

"Eat," she said, finally answering his question. "I want to eat my salad and my spaghetti, and then I want to have a glass of wine."

"You can have a dessert, too," he said.

"I won't have room for dessert."

"You don't have a sweet tooth?" he asked.

"I just have regular teeth."

He flashed her a happy smile, and she gave him a happy smile back.

Despite all the bad things that happened today, right now she felt happy. And she knew why. Because of Rob. She'd made a friend.

Then she looked at his lips again, and she warmed inside. And she thought maybe she'd made more than a friend.

Rosa Fabrini stopped by with their glasses of wine. She stayed to chat with them for a minute. Nia liked Rosa, who owned the restaurant with her chef husband. The few times Nia had spoken to Rosa, she'd been nice. She didn't treat Nia as if she were odd.

When Rosa left, Nia leaned forward and crossed her forearms on the table. "Justine hates me. She might've been the one who ran me over. With her in the hospital, I'm probably not in danger."

"Probably not." But he watched her closely, a frown puckering his forehead.

For the first time since she'd woken up in the hospital with her damaged brain, the silence compelled her to talk. "In that case, you don't have to stay with me anymore." As soon as the words came out of her mouth, so fresh she imagined them still hanging in the air between them like underwear on a clothesline, she wished them back into her mouth.

But it was true and she didn't want to lie to Rob. She didn't want to lie to anyone.

She'd lied too much in her old life. Maybe it was her lies that drove someone into running her over. Doing it not once but twice.

Now she had another chance. This time around, she was going to live a truthful life. Even if her truth was painful.

Since she probably wasn't in danger, Rob didn't have a reason to stay with her. He could go home. After all, she was lucky he'd spent so much time with her already. Especially since he wasn't really a constable.

Sometimes being a liar was okay. When you lied to

help someone else. Like Rob lied when he told her he was a constable. And maybe like Marc, her brother. Maybe he was helping someone else besides the people who wrote about him on the Internet. Maybe that's why he didn't visit and didn't call.

Maybe that's why he didn't write her a letter telling her how awful she was.

"Probably the other family members will come to visit Justine," he said.

Marc? Would Marc come to visit Justine?

Her chest tightened. Her throat closed

"Probably they will." She winced. Her voice sounded like a cartoon character's. "According to the computer, my sister and her husband are still married, though Justine doesn't use his last name in business. So he'll come. And my..." She frowned, the words in her mind stealing her happy moment.

"Father and mother," he said, the lightness wiped from his face. Replaced with grimness.

She nodded and told herself that none of it mattered. None of it.

But she lied to herself. It hurt inside her belly to think that her father and mother might have tried to kill her. That one or both of them had so much hate and anger toward her, they ran over her twice, just to make sure she was gone.

She reminded herself they were strangers to her. Nothing more. Maybe they were her biological parents, but with her memory gone, she may as well have been born out of a test tube.

"Yes," she said, her voice so soft that he frowned and leaned forward. She cleared her throat and picked up the glass of wine, telling herself it didn't matter. As long as they left her alone, none of it mattered. "They'll probably be there, too."

"In that case, there's a possibility you might be in danger."

"I might be." Not really, though. If they wanted to kill her already, they could've tried again. They knew where she lived.

But maybe they'd forgotten about her. Or maybe they were afraid. They got away with it once. Next time they might get caught.

"I should stay with you," Rob said.

Her breath caught in her lungs and the hand holding the glass trembled. She brought it to her lips and took a gulp. The wine was red and sweet and she took another gulp, even as she was aware that people didn't gulp down wine. At least not the people she watched on TV.

She set down the glass to keep from taking more swigs. Then she met his eyes, an unreadable brown, as if he were the blank page. But that was wrong. She was the one with the blank pages. Now some of the pages were filling up...and she didn't always like the words that were written on them.

"I think that would be a good idea," she said, her voice breathy. Once again, she felt as if someone had socked her in her belly. But this sensation wasn't hurtful, it was exciting. Like tiny fairies decided to use her belly as a dance floor.

Rob nodded, but his eyes blazed at her. For just one instant. Then the flare was gone and she picked up the glass and took another swig.

Because she suddenly felt like she needed it.

NINETEEN

Bast was not talking to Nia.

When the humans finally returned home, waking Bast from a nap, Nia was different. Breathless. She laughed softly, in a husky voice. And then there was the mating smell. It had thickened. Nia stank of it.

So did Rob.

Did Nia think Bast couldn't smell them? They may as well shout out what they wanted to do. Do a song and dance while they were at it. Naked. Their furless skin unclothed for anyone to see and touch and, above all, to mate.

Instead of greeting Nia with a meow and marking her the way she usually did, Bast remained curled on the bed. She'd walked through the streets of Miracle today to satisfy her curiosity. It had been invigorating and her curiosity still wasn't satisfied. But a cat needed her nap.

And when she'd returned home, Nia hadn't been there to greet her and Bast had to get into the house by pushing open the small door in the back that Nia had made for Bast's use so she could go in and out when she pleased.

But what she pleased most was for Nia to let her in and out. For Nia to be there whenever Bast wanted, for whatever Bast wanted.

Bast supposed she would forgive Nia. After all, Nia

couldn't help being human. And she couldn't stop her body from going into mating mode. Those things happened to almost all animals.

While Rob used the bathroom, Nia came to Bast and knelt next to the bed. She rested her forearms on the mattress and leaned so her face was only inches from Bast's. Her eyes were wide and different. Not quite still. As if thoughts buzzed in her brain like bees around flowers. Excitement streamed from her skin. She even breathed faster than normal, and Bast heard her heartbeat pound like a fast rain.

"Rob is going to stay with us tonight," Nia said. "He's guarding us."

Bast expressed her indignation with a loud mrrrreeeeooow. A word that if it were translated to English and were on TV, would immediately be covered with a loud beep.

Nia winced but didn't attempt to defend herself. Nia was too smart for that. One of the reasons Bast stayed with her.

Bast spoke again in a string of meows and mreows and other sounds that were too fast and too complex for most human ears to hear and understand. Even Nia frowned, as if trying to keep track of it all.

"We don't need a man to guard us," Bast told Nia in her indignant tirade. "Who warned you this morning about the intruder outside? Me! I warned you. It wasn't Rob. It wasn't any man."

"I'm sorry." Nia said, but she didn't look sorry. If she were a feline, she'd be purring. "You are brave and wonderful, and you can hear one hundred times better than a human—"

Nia mreeeooowed. "I can hear many, many, many times better than one hundred times." Nia wasn't sure how much one hundred meant, but it didn't matter.

"I know," Nia said, "but I'll feel more secure with Rob in the house."

The toilet flushed, and Nia sat back, lifting her arms from the bed. "It won't be for long," she said.

Bast felt a great sadness as Nia's face got all soft and Rob's heavy footsteps headed toward the bedroom. There was nothing Bast could do to stop Nia's foolishness. She may as well try to stop the sun from shining in the daytime or the moon at night.

The door opened and Nia got to her feet, then headed toward Rob, her eyes starry.

His eyes looked hungry, as if he were starving for her.

Bast turned her back on them. She could guess what they were going to do, and it wasn't anything interesting to her. She'd had a full day, and another nap sounded good right now. If she woke up before they were finished with their mating – because humans were so much slower doing *everything* than cats – Bast could always listen for creatures.

While they slept tonight, someone would need to watch the house in case the intruder came back.

It certainly wasn't going to be Mr. Stinking of Sex. She knew what was on his mind right now, and it wasn't protecting Nia. He didn't seem like a bad man, but Bast didn't know him yet. She wasn't about to put her scent on him.

If he wanted her trust, he needed to earn it.

And maybe, after the mating was over – which never seemed worth all the drama that followed – Nia would realize life was better without him.

After all, Nia had Bast, who was a much better companion than any man.

TWENTY

The loud notes of Tim McGraw's "Real Good Man" jerked Rob out of a dream. Only it wasn't a dream. Nia and he were in the living room. It was his suggestion to move there. If they had stayed in the bedroom, what happened there would not be conducive to sleep.

And the cat had been glaring at him. As if Bast knew what was in his mind every time he looked at Nia.

Before the phone rang, Nia had been leaning toward him, her face shiny, her lips parted, her eyes glowing. She was sitting on the flowered couch that didn't look anything like her. She wasn't the flowery type, unless it was one big flower. With a stamen, perhaps. Brightly colored and fragrant to attract hummingbirds and bees.

And Rob. He would fight the bees for her. He would wave off the hummingbirds.

Sitting across from her on a blue chair, he leaned toward her. Then shifted to the edge of the cushion.

If he edged forward any more, he'd have to get up and—

The damn phone rang.

A denial arose in Rob's mind. A wail of anger. He felt pulled to Nia by an invisible string that was attached to both of them and his brother picked a damn inconvenient time to—

The "Real Good Man" notes rang out again.

She looked at him with her eyes wide. "I think you have a phone call."

"It's Jerry," he said aloud. In his mind, he snarled out a few more words, none of them complimentary to his brother. He unhooked the cell from his belt and brought it to his ear. "Yeah."

"Nice way to answer the phone," Jerry said. "Don't tell me I interrupted anything."

"I won't. This better be good."

"I'm always good."

"That's not what Mom would say."

Jerry laughed. "Hey, who's the constable, huh?"

"That's because the voters don't know you as well as I do." Aware of Nia's stare, he looked back at her. She didn't glance away and pretend not to overhear. Instead she continued to watch him with her lips parted. As if he were a favorite TV show and she were an enthralled audience member.

"What've you got?" Rob asked.

"Not so fast," Jerry said. "I want a few answers, too."

Rob sat back on the chair that was too feminine for him, too small and a foaming sea-blue instead of a regular blue. He supposed some regular guys would like it, but he didn't want colors that reminded him of foam unless he was in a bath. And not alone, either. He wanted to be in the bath with—

Rob shut off his thoughts. "Then ask the questions," he said. Jerry was too fond of playing games.

"Bad timing?" Jerry asked.

"Just ask the damn question."

"In a hurry, are you?" Jerry laughed.

"You want me to hang up?"

"Watch how you talk to your older brother. I can still beat your ass."

"You never beat my ass. I'm a trained killer." He finally shifted his gaze from Nia. The invisible sex spell that connected them still shimmered but the connection was weaker now.

Because what he'd just told Jerry was something he didn't like to think about. Something he never talked about.

He'd killed. He wasn't lily white. He wasn't even gray.

There was dirt on his soul. That's why the cloud came. That's why he didn't deserve to be happy. Why he didn't deserve Nia.

" I'll give you one more chance before I hang up," he said, but could hear the change in his voice. The tiredness. The melancholy.

"You sound serious." Jerry's voice roughened. "Where are you? You haven't been home all day."

Rob wanted to tell him that was none of his business. When Jerry disappeared for the evening and didn't take his constable calls, Rob didn't ask where he was all night. But he was used to Jerry disappearing. Jerry wasn't used to him disappearing. Rob probably stuck to his home as much as Nia stuck to hers.

"I'm with Nia," Rob said. "Her family's in the area, and I don't trust them."

"Jesus, that's some kind of family. Makes ours look functional."

"It is. We had Mom. She took care of us."

"And Grandpa and Grandpa. And Dad was okay."

"When he was sober." Rob glanced at Nia and saw her frown. He looked away again. Someday he'd meet someone with a perfect life. It just hadn't happened yet. "I'm staying to make sure no one tries to break into Nia's house."

"You don't know that anyone was there last night to

harm her. The noise could've been a deer. Could've been kids. Could've been anyone."

"We know someone tried to kill her back in Minnesota. You can't deny that."

"It doesn't mean you have to go Sir Galahad on her."

"I was in Afghanistan for three and a half tours. I can handle anything that happens in Miracle."

"A bullet can be just as deadly in Miracle as in Kabul."

Rob watched Nia's expression grow sadder with each word, her eyes looking down, her lips pulled tight. With her sharp hearing, she heard every word he and Jerry said, and every inflection.

"That's enough." Rob's grip on the phone tightened. "I don't need a babysitter. If that's all you've got—"

"Dammit, don't hang up on me."

"Then get to the damn point."

"I did ruin your evening," Jerry said, proving the twin bond still worked between them. And as usual, proving it at an inconvenient time.

"'Bye," Rob said and clicked off the phone. Still holding it in his hand, he looked at Nia. "I still don't know why Jerry called. He's got issues."

"A woman?" Nia asked.

Rob shrugged, feeling a pang for his brother.

And a pang for himself.

Though their dad hadn't been the best parent in the world, they always knew he loved them. He gave his mother money for them most of the time, as far as he knew. And most of the time, his dad he was a happy drunk, though even happy drunks didn't have happy families. But they could've been worse.

So what happened to him and Jerry? Why were their lives so screwed up?

"Are you a mind reader?" he asked.

She shook her head, her expression serious. "Oh no."

He quirked up one side of his lips. He couldn't brood forever. He hadn't killed any children or women. Some things he had to do to keep his men safe.

Anyone in his unit would've done the same thing.

If it happened all over again, he'd do it again.

He'd joined the army, after all, not a church choir.

The notes from "Real Good Man" sang out again, and Rob put his phone to his ear. "What is it?"

"Her parents and husband are at the hospital," Jerry said. "They're staying in Tomahawk. So be careful."

"I'm always careful." Rob looked at Nia again, and she was looking back now, frowning slightly.

"Is that right?" Jerry's voice was mocking. "You brought condoms with you?"

Nia's eyes widened, her lips shaped in an *O*, then she glanced down at her lap, away from him.

Rob wished Jerry could be teleported to Nia's living room so Rob could slug him. "It won't be necessary. Goodbye."

He clicked the phone off. Nia glanced up, her eyes startled.

"I'm sorry," he said. "My brother's an asshole."

"And one of my family members might be a killer."

His shoulders relaxed and he breathed deeper. Good. Jerry hadn't screwed up his night permanently. With another woman, Rob wouldn't have worried. But Nia wasn't a normal woman.

"You win the worst relative award," he said. "I'm just glad you're not bothered by what he was saying."

"I think you should call him back."

He frowned. "You want to know more about your sister?"

"No, I want him to bring the condoms."

TWENTY-ONE

Rob stared at Nia for a long moment, and she felt her skin come to life. As if it had been sleeping and woke up with an extra burst of energy. The nerve ends quivered, waited for his touch. Wondering how it would feel.

She'd watched TV and read books, and had an idea what would happen.

Until she met Rob, sex had sounded less appealing than having a needle in her vein when the hospital technician took blood from her. Maybe the needle was better. It was certainly faster. Or so she thought.

But now...well, now, she didn't want fast. She thought she would prefer slow. Very, very slow.

Without saying a word, he pressed something on his phone, then held it to his ear and continued to stare at her while the phone rang on the other end.

She didn't take her gaze from his, either. They were locked into each other's stare like two cats. Then she heard Jerry answer and Rob said, "Bring the condoms."

She blinked, noting he said *condoms* plural.

"And my sketchpad and drawing pencils," Rob added.

"Your paints, too?" Jerry asked, his voice tinny.

"I don't think I'll use them, but throw them in." Rob's face still didn't show his emotion, but his eyes were lit, brilliantly alive. The way Nia felt inside. As if hundreds of fireflies flapped their wings inside her.

He hung up and stood. He held out his hands.

Slowly, she stood. Slowly, she stepped toward him.

It felt to her as if somewhere in her damaged brain she'd known from the first sight of him on the doorstep that this was how they'd end up. Together. Making love. Inevitable. That even as she consciously thought he was a liar and too thin, the cells of her body were seeing him with their own invisible senses, thinking *Yes. Him. This is the one we've been waiting for.*

They stood chest to chest. The contact took her breath away. His solid chest, belly, and thighs radiated warmth and strength. A man to lean against who wouldn't drop her or harm her. He would just...treasure her.

Her breath started again and so did the part of her that examined and categorized. The part she couldn't seem to shut off for long. Not even now as she noted his arms held her just right. Firm but not tight. Close but not suffocating. His head lowered, and she pushed up on her tiptoes, yearning for his kiss. Her first.

It didn't matter that she'd been kissed before the brain injury. She wasn't the same woman. She'd lost her memories. Now she was making new ones. Good ones. The best ever.

The second their lips touched, she started to shake and didn't know why. He was a gentle kisser, his lips soft, his chin slightly rough but the slight scratchiness felt...nice.

He raised his head. "Do you want me to stop?"

Under her fingers, she felt a slight tremor. He was shaking, too. Not because he feared her, she knew, but because he cared.

A sense of wonder – *happiness* – shot through her.

She put her hand to his face, held it against the warm

skin. "At Rosa's restaurant, you asked me what I wanted to do. I wasn't sure then what I wanted. But *this*..." She smiled at him, and it felt like the sun was a nimbus around them, wrapping them in warmth and light. "This I'm sure of."

His swift smile came out, then his head slanted down, his eyes lidded, and their parted lips met again. Her eyes closed, too, and for once she stopped thinking and she stopped cataloging. Instead, she just *felt*.

When he pulled away, she moaned her protest. But he stepped back, his hands gripping her upper arms. Slowly she exhaled and smiled at him.

"You don't have to stop."

"I do." His voice was husky. "Jerry will be here in a minute or two." He touched the side of her face, and ran his fingertips lightly down to her jaw.

She drew in her breath, then leaned her head against his breastbone and listened to the strong beat of his heart.

I want you, it pounded out. *I want you.*

With her mouth, she formed the words but didn't say them aloud. *I want you back.*

They stayed like that even as she heard a car coming down the street. A moment later, the car turned into her driveway. Rob lifted his head, finally hearing the soft purr of the car engine and the sound of the tires rolling on her driveway.

He kissed her forehead. "I'll be right back."

She headed toward the hall. He'd told her to make a decision and she was making one now that she didn't think she'd regret.

"I'll wait for you in the bedroom."

She remembered the story about the big, bad wolf. One of the folklore stories that her first therapist said would be a good idea to read.

"The better to eat you," the wolf had said to Little Red.

She had a more fitting phrase. *The better to love you.*

Nia's shining face with her eyes so trustful remained in Rob's mind like a beacon, pulling at him to hurry back inside even as Jerry stood on the front porch and scowled. Not looking like the happy-go-lucky twin right now.

"Be careful," Jerry said. "She's not the most stable person in the world."

"Then we make a combustible pair, because neither am I." Rob plucked the package from his twin's fingers, stepped inside, closed the door, locked it, then hurried to where Nia waited for him.

A song ran through his head, *"Feels like the first time."*

Remembering the first time he'd had sex, he grinned and a bit of his intensity slipped away. He sure the hell hoped it wasn't like the first time. Not with Allie Marren's big sister interrupting them, so he had to hide under Allie's bed for an hour. Not the most comfortable place for a fifteen-year-old with a hard-on.

In the hall before going up the staircase, Bast appeared before him. The slender, gray-shaded tortoiseshell cat meowed up at him in a string of up and down sounds that sounded emphatic.

"I won't hurt her," Rob said, though he didn't believe the cat could really talk to him.

The cat craned its neck further up at him and meowed again, this time the sounds shorter and even more emphatic. Rob could've sworn the cat said, *You better not!*

After giving Rob the devil's eye that said if he hurt Nia, he would pay, Bast padded down the steps, her head and her tail up.

Rob shook his head, curved his hand around the balustrade and sprinted upward. He wondered if Nia could hear his heart thunder. When he walked into her bedroom, the first thing he saw was her slender body on the bed, unclothed.

His heart twisted even as his body responded. Christ, she was lovely.

Looking at him, she half smiled, as if she held her breath while watching his reaction.

"You're beautiful." He croaked the words out, his throat tightening with an overload of emotion. So much desire.

He wasn't used to seeing so much beauty. Wasn't used to being so lucky.

It felt like a long time had passed since he woke up this morning, thinking it was going to be another day that he needed to plod through without tearing up any of his brother's property.

"My doctor tells me I'm too thin," Nia said.

"Mine tells me the same thing. I think you're perfect."

"Take off your clothes." She pushed up on her elbows, her upper body slanted, her small but full breasts sliding down a little. "I'll tell you what I think of you."

He put the condoms on the bedside table and started stripping. He was aware that the bed was full-sized rather than king or even queen. He was aware that the cover had a paisley design, the colors purple, pink, and turquoise. Colors Miriam might have picked out, not Nia. He was aware that the headboard was cherry wood and kind of beautiful yet old-fashioned.

And he was aware of the lacey drapes that filtered in the sunlight, giving the room a hazy, dreamy look.

It felt like a dream to him. And for a second fear froze him in place, with one jean leg off and one on. Afraid this whole day had been some kind of a weird dream.

But he looked at her again and the rush of blood in his body heated him. Stepping out of the other leg, he told himself that it didn't matter. If this were a dream – something the PTSD conjured up – he never wanted to wake up to reality.

Once undressed, he laid down next to Nia. Still on her back, she turned her head to gaze into his eyes. He kissed her, just their lips touching. Then their tongues. Sweet, so sweet. Sweeter than honey.

He wasn't going to do this quickly.

It was going to be slow and long and wonderful.

He pulled away and touched her. Not in a hurry. Letting his hand glide over her skin, starting with her shoulder then moving downward. Her beauty stunned him. He was honored to be here with her.

He told her so in a whisper as he still touched her, his fingers below her waist now, moving downward.

"Me too," she whispered back.

A small smile tipped up the corners of her lips. He gazed into her eyes. They shimmered, star-shot, as if a waking dream filled them. As his fingers slid lower, her eyes half lidded and her breath came out ragged.

Then his hand dipped between her legs, and her eyes opened wide and her lips parted wider. He stopped touching. He stopped breathing.

"Don't stop," she whispered, shaking her head.

Breathing again, harshly, he started again. She was damp and warm. A moan came from her throat that turned into a keen and another keen and then another again.

She touched him back, her fingers around his erection tentative, as if afraid of hurting him. He wanted to tell her to hold him harder because this light touch was killing him. Teasing him.

He was ready. Past ready. Ever since he'd seen her naked he'd been ready. Hell, he'd been ready since the first time she opened the door and told him her cat was talking to him.

Her breath hitched, her body trembled, her eyes closed. Another keen came out of her mouth. When she finished this time, she unclasped her hand from his erection then grabbed his hand that was touching her.

"Are you ever putting that condom on?" she asked.

He laughed, a great joy welling inside him. "Yes," he said. "Yes, yes, yes."

TWENTY-TWO

She watched him stand and roll the condom over his penis. He was so beautiful it made her ache. Just another part of the ache in her body that sent messages of *want* and *joy* and *delight*.

And *hurry*. She wanted him to *hurry* and touch her again.

He knelt on the bed, the mattress depressing. She watched his face as he looked at her, and a glaze came over his face. As if he were looking at her with his senses as well as his eyes.

As she looked at him, she felt the same thing.

He was...beautiful. His body more muscled than it appeared clothed. He could be a statue. If he were, she would want it life-sized in her bedroom. And his penis...she would want that life-sized, too. So she could look at the statue and never, ever forget this time together.

Yet despite these thoughts and feelings, a small fear remained in her. An apprehension that tightened inside her body like a spring about to pop up.

He lay next to her, and his face changed. Reforming from expectation to gentleness. As if he read the fear in her face and was reacting to it. Answering it. He reached out and put his hand on her ribcage.

A safe place.

She closed her eyes and her breath exhaled softly.

Before, the urgency had kept her from experiencing fully what she was doing. She'd felt with her body only. Now she felt with her heart as well as body.

His hand moved, his skin feeling thicker than hers. Warmer. A man's hand, everything bigger.

His palm and long fingers curved around her breast, and her breath hitched.

So this was what it felt like to have a man touch her there. Yes. Oh yes.

She closed her eyes. She knew from the letters and from talks with her counselors and therapists that she was not a virgin. Far from it. But with her reformatted brain, she was a virgin emotionally if not physically. This was a new experience. A wonderful experience.

His hand moved again, a slow slide downward. Slow, slow, slow. Pleasure shot through her nerve endings with every tiny slide of his hand. She wanted to close her eyes and just feel. But if she closed her eyes, she would miss watching his intense expression. Would miss seeing the joy in his face. The immense pleasure. As if he felt as much as she did. And she would miss the deepened brown of his eyes, almost black with passion. A color that matched the color of her hair.

She wanted him to match her everywhere.

She wanted to take a mental snapshot of him and file the image in her brain. Store it in a corner where she'd never forget this night. Because forgetting this would be a crime. She wanted to use her mind as a computer and tap on it whenever she felt the need to bring up this photo of him. She wanted to relive this moment, this second. She wanted to never forget it. Never, ever.

His hand slid below her waist.

She arched up.

"You like this?" he asked, and his voice was a rough

whisper.

"Oh, yes," she whispered back.

Then he slid his hand down her belly and he kept going until his fingers and palm covered her between her legs. She knew he was feeling her moistness and his hand moved in ways that made it even more wonderful. Made her arch higher. Made her eyes close. Made her want him. Want him. Want him. Want him.

"Oh yes," she said. "Oh yes, oh yes, oh yes."

His leg crossed over hers, and he pushed up against her, the length of his condom-wrapped erection pressed against her hip. "I can't wait any longer."

She opened her eyes, turned toward him. She wanted to smile, but the feeling was too big for a smile. Too burning.

"Don't wait," she said. "I don't want to wait any longer."

He rolled on top of her, one leg on either side, then slid in, a strained look on his face as if he were in pain.

"Tell me if I'm hurting you," he said.

She reached up for his arms. "You're not hurting me."

Before she finished speaking, he slid inside slowly and she felt the lovely stretch of her muscles and skin and, oh, the slide of him.

The glorious slide.

The wonder.

And then the joy, exploding inside her. Like fireworks. She closed her eyes and hung on tightly.

TWENTY-THREE

Nia stretched, her eyes still shut, waking slowly, her body languorous and heavy and delicious, instead of coming awake with her usual morning spurt of nervousness then pushing it down. Reminding herself that she made her own life.

But not today. Today she just felt...wonderful.

Now she understood why people talked so often about sex. Why women dressed to attract men. Why men turned their heads to watch women when they passed them. Why men and women did stupid things even when they knew they were being stupid.

All because of this wonderful, wonderful feeling.

She opened her eyes to the morning sun flooding into the room, onto her bed. She'd slept later than usual. Rob was sitting on the rocking chair in the corner, wearing only his briefs, sketching.

"So, it wasn't a dream," she said. A lovely dream. The best dream. Someone treating her as if she were something precious.

He didn't talk for a moment. She started to swing her legs to the side, and his head shot up. "Don't move."

"Why not?" she asked, unmoving for now.

"So I can finish the lines."

"You'd better hurry. I need to use the bathroom."

"I need to draw you," he said, drawing furiously.

"One minute."

"Five."

"One."

"Four."

"One."

"Three."

"Two."

He glanced up from his drawing pad. "You compromised to make me feel better?"

"Yes." She didn't crack a smile. In her observance of men, she'd concluded they were like dogs while women were like cats. Like dogs, you had to throw men a treat now and then.

And women...women needed to be valued. Often. Any chance men got, they should value women.

An ache started within her and she didn't know why. After all, Rob had valued her last night. He was still valuing her this morning.

"What's the matter?" Rob asked, his voice sharp.

She looked at his face and saw his frown that wasn't really angry. It was a frown that said he cared what she was feeling. Cared enough to read her face the way she was reading his.

"I just got sad."

"About what?"

She shook her head. Probably not a good idea to tell him her *men are like dogs, women are like cats* theory. She'd only told Dr. Whitcomb about it and he hadn't appreciated it. Nia suspected the doctor liked to think of himself as a cat. He had a few feline qualities but mostly—

A new thought popped into her mind, silencing the old one. As if it had always been there, waiting for the right time to come out and announce itself.

Chilled, she threw off the cover and jumped out of

bed. Rob didn't say anything, though she didn't think the two minutes of stillness that she'd agreed to were up.

In her peripheral, his face changed, looking stern. His eyes darkened with concern.

She hurried into the bathroom across the hallway. She saw by the damp bath towel that he had already showered. She took one as well, though she wanted to keep the remnants of his scent on her. But she knew that was silly.

In people, unlike cats and dogs, natural smells weren't desired, except perhaps ones from bottles. It was a matter of protection to smell like the others. To blend in.

Now more than ever.

When she returned to the bedroom, Rob was gone and Bast was rubbing her scent on her bed, overlaying hers and Rob's.

Nia sat on the side of the bed and curved her hand over the top of Bast's small head. Bast pushed her head harder against Nia's palm and meowed a demand for a good rub.

"I guess I won't need to change the sheets now," Nia said out loud.

Bast meowed her agreement.

"I guess I should thank you."

Bast meowed her agreement again.

"Thank you very much." Nia got up and headed to the dresser for her clothes. She heard dishes in the kitchen downstairs. She hadn't worried about where Rob had gone, not consciously, but a small tightness inside her eased.

Knowing Rob was in her house, she breathed easier. She felt *right*. As if the world had tilted the wrong way and now it was okay again.

Her clothes on, she hurried downstairs. Bast padded behind her. A new day, a new adventure.

The new day part, Nia liked.

New adventure...not so much. She'd had enough adventures already. It would be nice to have a day with the only adventures exploring Rob's body.

Once downstairs, she established with Rob that she drank tea and not coffee. From the flicker in his eyes, she could tell he liked coffee.

She made a note to buy coffee and a coffee maker. Just a small one, because he might not stay.

The thought made her chest squeeze, and she shut it down.

Sometimes it was better not to think.

While he made eggs and toast, she started the tea, making enough for two. They ate in silence, so quietly the lap of Bast's tongue in her water bowl sounded loud.

When Nia finished eating, she took her cup to the living room and looked out the big window at the trees and the tangled bushes. At flowers growing wild that she needed to tame.

But not now. Untamed looked good to her now. She opened the front door and stepped out onto porch, to the railing. Standing there, she inhaled the fresh air, the smell of trees and flowers and earth and sky. The smell of life.

Rob followed her out and stood next to her. "What changed you this morning?" he asked.

She stared at a purple flower that was probably a weed. Forcing her shoulders not to flinch. Her body not to tighten.

She'd known he would ask. She hadn't been ready to talk about it before. Now she was ready. "I thought of something Dr. Whitcomb said."

Rob made a grunt of derision.

Nia gazed down at her tea. "He said that with my brain damage and complete loss of memory, I was like a newborn."

She could see Rob nod in her peripheral. "And I quickly became like a child." Rob nodded again, and she continued. "Then he said a well-nurtured child looks at the world as a place of potential delight and I look at it as a place that could hurt me."

"You were hurt," he said.

"Yes, but if I didn't remember the experience of being hurt, I should have been...happier. Instead I was... I don't know. Fearful." She frowned, because she liked to think of herself as brave. Strong. Surviving on her own.

But when she thought of her family...the letters, the silence, the visit from her sister...

The person that ran her over twice...

She shuddered, as if a snake with cold and slippery scales crawled along her flesh. Rob's arm curved around her shoulders, his support giving her the sense that he wouldn't let anyone harm her.

She closed her eyes and allowed herself to lean against him. He was her haven, her safe place.

But she couldn't stay like this forever.

Slowly she opened her eyes, then straightened and looked into his intense gaze. "Do you think we should investigate?"

He nodded. "We could go to the hospital. Talk to your sister, your mother, your father. Is that what you want?"

A shiver made her suck in her breath. She exhaled, then sipped her tea. It warmed her. So did the knowledge that Rob was at her side, listening to her. "Now that I know so much, I suppose I should." Another shiver attacked her, and she shook her head. "But I don't want to see them."

"Good. I don't, either."

His comment surprised a laugh out of her. The corners of his lips tipped up, but his eyes remained sad and watchful. Her laughter shut down but she smiled back, a great well of affection for him rising inside her.

Later, she would act on that affection. She'd been avoiding this other mess ever since she was in the hospital and learned she had a family that despised her.

But with her sister's visit yesterday, the mess had come to her. And sometimes the best thing to do with a big mess was to roll up your sleeves and clean it up.

Which meant she should do this. She knew it, but it scared her.

Maybe start with someone who scared her the least. Someone whose name didn't make her shiver.

"I never got a letter from Marc," she said. "That makes me think he's the one I should talk to."

"Anyone else?"

"There's no one else." She shrugged her left shoulder. "One of my family members might have harmed me. If it happened, I want to know. If I know, maybe I can...convince them to leave me alone. I'll warn them if they try again, they'll be in very big trouble."

"What about punishment?" His eyes darkened, his face grim. Scary grim. "Whoever hurt you should pay for what they did."

She stared into his eyes, and she spoke slowly, putting weight into every word. Because what she said was her truth. And the truth was not something to say with lightness. "I want them to go away and never come back. That's all I want."

He touched his fingers to her lips and outlined them, as though he were painting them. "You're a rare person."

"I know." Then despite the tension in the room, she smiled. What he called *rare*, others called *weird*.

Getting to know him was the best thing that happened to her since she woke up in the hospital and didn't know where she was or who she was.

He laughed. "Anyone else would want revenge. That accident tore up your life."

She lifted her hand to his neck, let her fingers draw across it. Felt the tightness of his skin. Felt the cords and the muscles. Felt the heat. "I don't think it was a good life."

"Are you going to make a better life? Is that why you've been watching everyone? Seeing what to do and not to do?"

She liked the brown of his eyes. They were like the earth. They grounded her. They said *plant your heart here and you will flourish.*

Of course they didn't really say any of that. But she was sure if they could talk, that's what they'd say.

"Yes," she said. "Yes to everything you said." In reality, she was studying people to see how to act like them. So she wouldn't be different.

But the truth was she would always be different. And what she really wanted was a better life, even if it were different from everyone else's.

"Your family is toxic. You're sure you want to do this?" He lowered his head.

She watched him in fascination. His breath was warm on her skin. "I'm not sure of anything." Except this. Kissing him. Making love with him. Their arms around each other. Their bodies joined. "I suspect they would lie anyway."

"And upset you." His head lowered closer to hers. And closer yet. Their lips met and clung for a long moment.

He pulled back. "I wouldn't want anyone to upset you."

"Then you shouldn't stop kissing me until this is over, or my body will be very upset."

TWENTY-FOUR

Nia's crooked smile made Rob's belly twist and his body react. For at least the fiftieth time since he woke up this morning, he thought of the four condoms in his back pocket, courtesy of his twin.

He stepped back. "I'll call your brother."

They needed to get this straightened out. Once that was done, they could go back to the loving.

If she still wanted to. He had the feeling that the hate her sister had spewed and the anger he'd seen in the letters was just a small part of the horror behind her previous life. Like the gray clouds that came before the storm.

And like a storm, this could be destructive.

She nodded slowly. "Let's do it." She turned to go inside.

He followed her, frowning. Another twist in his belly told him something bad was going to happen.

The last time he'd had a feeling like this, he'd ended up in a V.A. hospital with a concussion and a burst eardrum, the memory seared in his brain of the unseeing eye of his best friend whose wife just had a baby the week before. And on his other side was T. J., his plans of starting a music studio with his cousins in their small Tennessee town blown up on a rock-hard Afghanistan road.

Rob hadn't been able save them.

This time he would do better.

The screen door shut behind him and he turned to lock it. Nia watched him, her expression solemn. As far as he knew, no one locked their doors in Miracle.

That was changing now, at least for Nia.

"I'll get Marc's phone number from the Internet," she said.

Two minutes later, he listened to the rings on a cell phone. Voice mail answered, letting him know he'd reached Marc Beaudine Construction and to leave a message.

"This is Rob Ackerman from the village of Miracle, Wisconsin. Your sister Nia lives here. Someone ran over her twenty-one months ago, causing massive memory loss." He kept his eyes on her. Except for a tensing of her jaw, she didn't react. She stood with her chin up and took it like a soldier.

He turned his gaze away from her. It was easier to talk when he wasn't watching her reaction to what he was saying.

"Your sister Justine came over here yesterday, bringing a gun. She's in the hospital now with an overdose." Listening to his words, Rob thought it sounded like an episode from a soap opera. Maybe that's what life really was, though for most people the episodes moved a little slower. "Your family is in the area now, visiting Justine. Considering the vitriol in letters they sent Nia, it's possible one of them was the person who tried to kill her. Having them so near makes us uncomfortable. We'd like to talk to you."

He left his cell phone number, looking back at Nia. Her eyes were wide. It felt to him that inside her chest, her heart was wide, too. Too wide, making herself a more visible target.

He paused to take a breath before saying goodbye. Instead he blurted out, "We fear for her life."

He hung up.

As soon as he did, she was in his arms, the phone clasped in his hand, Nia's slight body pressed against his chest.

He held on tight to both.

He was going to use the condom after all.

A burst of emotion shot off inside of him. It took a moment to recognize it: pure joy.

He'd been living with the stink of death in his heart for too long. Taking its toll on him. Making him wonder some days if life were worth living.

But when he was making love to Nia, every cell in his body was alive and damn glad of it.

Bast watched them sink onto the small couch in the office, their faces locked together, stinking of sex.

Not again. Already?

She made a hissing sound to show her displeasure, then turned her tail to them and trotted out of the office. Bast would never understand humans and was just glad she wasn't one of them.

While they were busy, she would patrol the house. Someone had to protect Nia, and it certainly wouldn't be this man who was too busy putting his mouth and other parts of his body all over her.

The wonder exploded inside Nia. A scream came out of her. And another. And another. Screams of joy. A joy so great she couldn't contain it inside her.

Sex the second time was even better than the first. No

apprehension. Just anticipation. Just holding. Just feeling. That slide inside her. And then out, and then in. And on and on. The small explosions of ecstasy making her clutch him and scream.

She stopped suddenly, gripping his shoulders.

He pushed up. His face tense.

"Am I hurting you?"

"No! You're making me feel wonderful." She felt lit up like a sunbeam. "Really, really wonderful. I want to do the same for you."

The muscles in his face relaxed slightly and his eyes darkened. "Next time."

"I don't want to be selfish." She'd been selfish in her previous life, and people hated her. She was having a new life now. A do-over. In this second chance, she was going to do things differently.

"You gave me pleasure last time," she said. "I want to give you pleasure this time."

"I had pleasure last time." He grinned then lowered his head to kiss her on a sensitive place that made her eyes close and her breath hiss.

And inside her, he twitched. He grew.

"Pleasure like this," he said, his voice thick.

She opened her eyes and he was smiling at her, so much tenderness in his gaze that her heart squeezed tight and so did her throat. And the joy inside her. It doubled. Tripled. Exploded again.

And she knew then that giving him pleasure would just increase her own delight.

He lowered himself, and she wrapped her legs around his thighs. *Next time,* she thought.

Then she rolled him so he was on the bottom. All because a question had intruded into her mind.

What if there were no next time?

TWENTY-FIVE

"**I**'m going to call your brother again."

Nia rolled out of bed and grabbed tissues to wipe her inner thighs. The lingering I-feel-fabulous glow flickered out. She didn't know a lot about after-sex talk and she didn't think Rob did, either.

"I'll call him," she said.

"You sure?"

She started pulling on her clothes, not looking on him, tension pulsing through her blood. If she looked at him, she might back down. This was something she needed to do. "I can talk to him."

His hand curved around her shoulder and she heard his inhale and exhale behind her. The scent of lovemaking hung in the room. Her nostrils flared, and she smelled the distinctive scent of his body. She wanted to lean back against him, melt into him.

But she was made of muscles and bones, and muscles and bones didn't melt easily. She had a backbone for a reason.

"I've been living alone for months and managing," she said. But her voice didn't sound confident to her own ears. It sounded like the voice of someone who was doing something she didn't want to do. "I can manage this, too."

"I know you can. I just want to help you."

It was tempting. Tempting not to just say yes, but to

sigh and slump against him. To turn and let his strong arms hold her. To let him protect her. Take care of her.

Instead she remained standing, her spine straight. He'd done enough. When she moved to Miracle, she was determined to be strong. She was determined to learn how to be a human. A good one. Not like the human she used to be. At least not according to the letters her family had sent her.

So far her best role model was her cat. At Wegner's, the only store in town where she could buy groceries and other necessities of life, Linda Wegner talked about everyone with a gleeful meanness that made Nia want to flee.

Anyone could be bad.

People gossiped, people lied, people cheated.

Besides Rosa Fabrini and now Rob, the most helpful person was the farmer that she heard grew "weed." It had taken a few minutes on the computer to find out that in addition to wild, unwanted plants, "weed" also meant marijuana. A different kind of weed that could be smoked and used medically. Or illegally, which was confusing to Nia.

So much of life was confusing. Maybe later it would make sense.

The farmer's daughter Katie – who appeared to be about Nia's age – was nice, too, though Nia didn't know her well. Nia wasn't ready to let anyone get close to her. Not until she learned how to be a better person.

But ready or not, it was time for Nia to stop watching the actions of other people. It was time for her to start acting. Time to be the best person she could be.

"I can handle it." Except for one wobble in her voice, she thought she sounded convincing.

Rob gave her shoulder a squeeze. "I know you can."

He kissed her shoulder, then she heard him step away, leaving her with a sense of strength. She felt braver because he believed in her.

She hadn't considered herself weak before. After all, she'd survived something horrible. But something in her brain felt different. Changed. Instead of thinking of herself as a survivor, she realized she was bold. An adventurer.

"You want to call him here?" he asked.

She glanced around. Not in the bedroom. She didn't want to taint her memories of last night.

Without a word, she headed to the kitchen for water, then carried the water and her phone to the couch in the living room, with the sun pouring in through the big window. Only then did she sit down.

Rob sat next to her, so close she could smell him but not quite close enough for their legs to touch. He said her brother's phone numbers out loud, and she punched them in. As the phone on the other end rang, a cowardly part of her, the same part that made her avoid looking straight into faces when she walked along the streets, thought it wouldn't be a bad idea if she got an answering machine or voice mail.

"Beaudine Construction," a man said, his voice firm and trustworthy. The kind of voice used to sell insurance on TV.

She knew it didn't really mean he was trustworthy. It just meant he *sounded* trustworthy.

Her stomach muscles contracted. Rob pressed his hand on her shoulder. Letting her know he was there for her.

She gave him a smile that she knew was shaky and looked away, remembering her newfound bravery, though most of it had fled.

"This is Nia Beaudine," she said and tried to make her voice as firm and steady as Rob's. She hoped Marc didn't hate her like the others, but she wasn't here for approval. She knew her own worth.

Most of the time, she knew it.

The other times she was sure she had no worth to anyone in the world accept her cat.

A silence came from the other end. She couldn't even hear any breathing.

"I'm your sister," she said.

"I know who you are."

"I live in—"

"I know where you live."

"Did you know that my...*our* sister Justine was here. She had a gun in her purse. I don't know if she planned to use it. She fell and the gun dropped from her purse, and she had to leave."

More silence came from the other end, but she heard quiet, shallow breaths. If this were a horror movie, she'd be scared. But it was real life, and real life was scarier than movies. Unlike a TV, she couldn't turn off it off. Or in a movie theater, get out of her seat and walk out.

If that were possible, she suspected a lot of people would walk out of their lives.

"Did you know she's in the hospital now?" she asked, even though he had to know. Unless he hadn't listened to Rob's message. Maybe the answering machine didn't work.

Maybe he was the one who'd tried to kill her.

"Not because of the fall," she said, her voice faltering, "but because of a drug overdose."

More silence with the rasps of breath. It was like being in the dark and knowing someone was nearby, just around the corner, even though she couldn't see or hear him.

"Do you care?" she asked.

"No."

But he was still there, still hanging on. He had to care a little. He even said one word. Not the word she wanted, but even a 'No' held hope.

If he didn't care, wouldn't he have hung up?

Anger flashed inside her body. Fast and hot and formidable.

Not at him. At herself.

Why was she agonizing over this? She hadn't called to find out if he held her in some kind of affection. She'd called to find out if he tried to kill her.

Or if not him, then who?

"I just want this to stop." She looked at Rob and he nodded, sending her silent encouragement. She took a deep breath and looked away from him. "I want to live my life without worrying that someone is going to try to kill me again." Her voice rose. "Is that too much to ask?"

She put her hand over her forehead, her neck curving forward. She frowned at her lap, as if her tan cotton pants offended her.

But that wasn't right. *Life* offended her. Life was hard.

Something landed on her head, wiping the thoughts from her mind.

Lips. Rob. He was kissing her softly on the crown of her head. Mere inches from where she'd been run over.

His lips left her head, and she looked up at him again.

She was not alone.

This man in her life... This was her miracle.

Maybe she should thank the intruder.

Except whoever it was didn't want to make her happy.

"Do you know that our parents and sister sent me letters when I was in the hospital?" She straightened her spine and her neck, speaking quickly to keep her voice matter-of-fact. "They wanted to explain why they weren't visiting me."

There was silence on the other end, but it wasn't dead air. Marc was still on the other end, listening.

"You didn't send a letter," she added, then winced. As if he didn't know what he did or didn't do.

"I kept track of your progress."

She wondered what that meant. Did Marc call the hospital every day? Did he stop by himself? No, if he'd done that, one of the nurses would have told her.

She gripped the phone harder.

"Do you..." She paused because this was an awful thing to ask. A stupid, needy thing that would make her cringe later. But knowing that it didn't matter. She had to try.

Her voice lowered to a whisper, she started again. "Do you care for me?"

She waited, hardly breathing. Next to her, Rob's breath was shallow, and she knew he waited, too.

No answer came. A silent cry started inside her and she shut it off. Not now. He hadn't hung up. She still had hope.

"Is that why you kept track of me?" she asked.

The waiting started again. One second...two seconds...three seconds... By this time, the other person was usually talking.

Then it hit her. He was doing the same thing she usually did. Waiting for her to talk first so he wouldn't have to say anything.

And another thought hit her. Conked her on the head like a hardball.

Maybe she didn't learn this thing about staying silent after she'd come to in the hospital with a wiped-out memory. Maybe this was something she'd learned a long time before that. The same time Marc learned.

"Were you hoping I'd die?" she whispered.

She started to rock back and forth on the couch, not realizing it until Rob's hand flattened on her back, reminding her that she wasn't alone. That he had her back.

Looking up at him, she mouthed *thank you*.

He smiled, and her heart stuttered.

A sudden storm of emotion twirled inside her. She couldn't identify it but she had to look away or she'd start crying. The churning feelings were too overpowering to think about right now.

Right now, it was about her and Marc. And her brother who might be the secret to her past.

"The letters all said why they hated me and the awful things I did," she said, her voice rough, driven on by desperation to keep him from hanging up. "My friend thinks all those terrible things I did were the classic behavior of someone suffering from PTSD. That stands for Post Traumatic Stress—"

"I know what that means." Marc's voice was harsh, and in that second she knew her hopes were false. She must've done something awful to him. Something he was thinking of right now.

Her hand twitched on the hard plastic of the phone, and she realized her palm was sweaty. She needed to stop agonizing over what might or might not have happened to her.

He knew what happened to her. His memories weren't stolen.

Just hers. Just the first twenty-five years of her life.

"Since I wasn't in a war and my behavior started so early," she continued, "he thinks I was abused when I was a child. Can you tell us...anything?"

There was a long silence on the other end. She bit her lip, reminding herself that if she remained quiet, he would fill the void. After all, he could have hung up, but he didn't. He was still listening.

"No," he said.

Then the phone went dead. She couldn't hear anything. Not even someone holding his breath.

And all she could think of that she hadn't asked him what really mattered.

Was he the person who'd sent her the Harry Potter books?

If he sent them, that meant he did care.

Just the thought that she might matter to him, that he might hold her in affection, filled her throat with stupid tears. She didn't know why. When bad things happened she faced them with her lips tight and chin up. But when it seemed someone might care about her...

Why did that make her blink back tears?

She turned to Rob, shaking her head, feeling oddly lost and alone. More than at the hospital when day by day went by and no one came.

It was all she'd known then. It was different now. Now she knew better.

"He said no." Nia set down the phone.

He looked her straight in the eyes. "Then we'll find another way."

She nodded. If he said there would be another way, she trusted he would find it. And he didn't say *he* would do it. He said *we*. That was even better.

But even with trust, she didn't have a clue how they would make it happen.

TWENTY-SIX

Rob had one trick up his sleeve. But it involved Nia's so-called family and he wanted to keep them away from her. He'd sooner open her front door to a pack of starving, feral wolves than her family.

They made his father look like a teddy bear.

And so far he'd only met two members of Nia's family. Three if he counted Miriam, but she'd left Nia the house, so he was inclined to think kindly of her.

While Nia made tea, he walked onto the porch and speed-dialed Jerry. He told his twin what he needed. Jerry put him on hold, then made a phone call to Debbie to find out if the other family members were around.

Rob's involvement started because of Jerry's job. May as well make use of it.

The moments ticked by. Rob watched a squirrel scamper across the lawn and a sparrow and a cardinal fly onto the branches of the crooked tree.

He wanted to paint the tree. Paint the birds. Paint Nia. Over and over. He pictured her. Saw her tentative smile, her wide eyes, her—

"Nia's sister is still at the hospital," Jerry said, taking Rob back to the half-wild, half-tamed front yard. "Debbie said Justine's husband and Nia's parents are staying at the lodge on Lake Nokomis. I called and the Beaudines are still checked in. That leaves me out. I can't go there and warn them off."

"Sure you can."

"Only if I want to end up in jail. This isn't a cop show on TV where they do whatever the hell they want. I have limits. You see me paired with a wise-cracking, sexy cohort who runs around in five-inch heels and is wildly attracted to me but can't commit because her mother was murdered when she was a kid? Hell no. I'm just a constable. My jurisdiction is limited to Miracle and no further."

Rob heard the roughness of Jerry's voice. Something wrong there again, but Rob couldn't handle Jerry's problems now.

"You're better than any of the TV cops," he said. "You're the real thing."

It was true in Rob's book. Especially now when he was fighting for Nia. Maybe for her emotional recovery. Maybe for her life.

Too bad for Nia that her champion needed his own emotional and mental sanity. Too bad for her that he had days – *weeks* – when he wondered why he survived when the others died.

He was like a tornado at a trailer park, and he lived in the one trailer that the tornado didn't touch. All shiny and intact with destruction and rubble all around it.

The dark cloud swirled down at Rob. Circling him. Touching him. Smothering him. Seeping into his throat, his lungs, his chest.

He folded his fingers into tight fists. No! He was not going into the darkness. He needed the light to be there for Nia.

Gritting his teeth, he imagined shoving the dark clouds away from his chest, then his throat and his head. He pictured them swirling out of the top of his head. Imagined them spinning away like tornadoes going in reverse, high up into the sky.

Nia. He had to think of Nia.

An image of her on the bed this morning as he drew her filled his mind. She lay on her back with her lips parted, her small, beautifully shaped breasts bared. Her pale skin iridescent in the morning sunlight, reminding him of the smooth surface of a pearl.

The last dark vapors evaporated. No room in his mind for darkness. Not with the picture of Nia in his mind, everything about her glowing: her skin, her eyes, her curved lips.

When this was over, he would paint her all day.

"You know you're out of your territory, but they don't," he said. "Put on your uniform, wear your gun, and they'll never suspect a constable isn't part of the sheriff's department. Once in, you can think of something to get information from them. Or scare them off for good, if that's what it takes. Use your imagination."

The words barely out of Rob's mouth, he scowled. He was telling the practical joker of the county to make something up. That was like giving an arsonist a box of matches, a gallon of gasoline, and pointing him to a barn during a drought.

"You in love with her?" Jerry asked.

"I hardly know her."

"You're not answering my question."

"When I hear a question I want to answer, maybe I will. I've got an idea. I'll wear your spare uniform and talk to them myself."

Jerry groaned. "Oh no. Not that. The way you're talking, you're going to do something really stupid."

"Listen to yourself," Rob said. "You're the one who usually does something stupid."

"Maybe so, but there are levels of stupid. I'm the

expert, you're the dunce. I don't get caught. And at least I'm not tilting at windmills."

"That's what windmills are for."

Jerry laughed, but it was rueful. The same kind of laugh he gave after Rob signed up for the army and he called Rob an idiot. "I'll do it. If you go, you'll give yourself away."

"You sure?" Rob asked.

"I said I'd do it." Jerry spoke faster, his tone energetic. "Maybe the family will be at the motel room before dinnertime. I have an old girlfriend who works at the hospital. I'll see if she's on tonight. She can be my spy."

Rob imagined the intent look on Jerry's face and the spark in his eyes. Jerry liked this kind of thing, the reason why he took the constable job instead of something that paid more. His only complaint was the people who called him in the middle of the night. Especially when he wasn't where he was supposed to be in the middle of the night.

Some might say he was committing his own crimes.

Some might be right.

Rob shook his head. Jerry knew what he'd gotten into when he started this. Rob didn't know the details, didn't want them, and didn't need them.

If anything happened to Jerry, Rob would be there for him. But right now it was Rob who needed Jerry. Right now it was Rob's story. More than that, it was Nia's story.

"They might be gone by now," Jerry went on. "The sister should be out of the hospital soon. I'm surprised they kept her overnight. Remember when Uncle Amos was in the hospital after the throat operation? They wanted him to go home the next day."

"How could I forget?" Rob laughed. "My favorite part

was when Aunt Donna threatened to get the bowling team, the snowmobile club, and four-wheelers to picket the hospital."

"She would've, too. Your girlfriend's sister must've been pretty bad off for them to keep her. I doubt they'll keep her another night."

"Just long enough so she has to pay for an extra day."

"Cynic."

Rob shrugged. He'd been in the military. He'd earned his cynic badge the hard way: small paychecks, long marches, and big bombs.

"I owe you." Rob heard the roughness in his voice. One day he'd make it up to Jerry. Since Rob had come home seven months ago, he'd been staying in Jerry's house, eating Jerry's food, upsetting Jerry's life. About time he made his own life.

"You coming home?" Jerry asked.

"Not while Nia's family is still around." Rob peered behind him at the house, the big window in the front reflecting his face and the tree that looked better than he did. "She needs me now."

"I'll be there soon." Jerry's tone turned serious, as if he sensed that Rob had changed.

"One more thing," Rob said.

"I should've known. There's always one more thing."

"Make it two more. Coffee. Get me coffee."

"She's not a coffee drinker?" Jerry laughed. "You getting withdrawal pains yet?"

"You forget where I was for four tours. I'm used to deprivation."

"'Used to' doesn't mean you gotta like it. What else?"

"Find out everything you can about her brother. Marc Beaudine. He's a contractor in Eau Claire. People on Emily's List like him, but that's all we know."

"I have a friend who's a deputy in the Eau Claire's sheriff's department. I'll ask her to look him up."

Rob nodded. Jerry had a lot of friends of the female kind. Females who remained friends after the break-up. Rob figured it was because they didn't expect anything of him when they started their relationship.

Their perception was Jerry's joy.

And it was Jerry's curse.

"Can you do it quickly?" Rob asked.

"I can't make promises. I have another friend who used to work for the D.A. in Eau Claire. She has a kid now and specializes in real estate law. I'll give her a call, too."

Rob nodded. "I owe you."

"Don't be stupid. I'll call you when I get anything."

They clicked off. Hooking the phone onto his belt, Rob crossed to the house and to Nia. Through the screen door, he heard her talking. "I don't know if he'll stay tonight."

Rob stopped and his heart leapt. *Yes, he would be here tonight.*

"Don't you like Rob?" she asked.

Rob frowned. Was she on the phone?

Bast meowed, then followed with a string of meows in up and down scales. As if the cat were indeed saying something to her. Rob listened, not sure how he felt about the cat talking to Nia or whether she really understood the cat.

It could be part of her brain damage – though there was nothing damaged about the woman in his arms last night. Or this morning.

Or it could be a symptom of her abuse. As far as Rob could see, Nia had no friends. He was it. No lovers since she moved to Miracle – except him. No family backup, either. Just an anonymous book giver who could be friend or foe.

Nia's life overflowed with question marks. No wonder she thought her cat was talking to her. No wonder she thought Bast might be the miracle that was prophesied.

And why the hell not? The world abounded with stuff no one understood. There were hormones in pretty much everything except Sam's weed. People were finding images of Jesus in apples and on bottoms of coffee mugs.

Why not a talking cat?

It was just too damn bad Bast wasn't a talking cat that could read people's minds. That would make it easier to find the would-be killer and the secret to Nia's past.

Nia was opening the screen door. "Bast said you weren't talking anymore. Her hearing is even sharper than mine. What did Jerry say?"

Rob stepped inside and turned to her in the hall. "He's going to check in on your family tonight."

She frowned. "You don't look thrilled."

"It's all we have," he said.

The frown cleared and she looked sideways at him. A coy look. "If it doesn't work, you could move in with me." She grinned. "To make sure no one kills me."

And then she laughed. For the first time since he'd known her, she seemed carefree and whole.

His breath caught. He wanted to capture this on canvas. This would be a picture he wanted to see every morning when he awoke.

Her laughter stopped abruptly, and a puzzled frown indented between her eyebrows, as if she wondered what had gotten into her.

He knew what had gotten into her. *Him.*

The thought that he could have such an effect on her filled him with power. In this intense twenty-four hours, they'd gotten to know each other and care for each other more than many couples who'd dated for months and even years.

He could see the change in her. The owning of herself and her sensuality. The new awareness. The new boldness.

When she first opened the door to him in his borrowed constable clothes, she'd been a pastel. Now she was an oil.

And she changed him, too. She gave him a purpose. She gave him hope.

No one was going to take that away from them. Take *her* away from him.

He told her Jerry's plan as she gazed at him, her eyebrows contracted slightly. He felt her total attention, as if it were a force.

She *was* a force. She was *his* force.

"I want to be there," she said.

"To talk to them?"

She looked away and inhaled, her small breasts rising and then falling. She turned back to him, her expression almost calm except for a muscle in her left cheek that twitched.

"I need to see them for myself." She frowned. "I don't know if I can talk to them, but I want to see their faces. I want to hear what they say. I deserve that much."

"It might be dangerous."

She nodded, her chin looking oddly stubborn. "I don't care."

He glanced down and saw her hands were clutched together.

He breathed out his frustration. "I'll let Jerry know. It looks like we're going on a road trip."

Her muscles relaxed and she broke out into the

biggest smile he'd seen her give. It made him think of a double rainbow. Or, better yet, sex.

Right now.

He took her hand and tugged her toward the bedroom. She laughed, and this time it seemed to come easily. He was teaching her to laugh.

And maybe to love.

Or was that what she was teaching him?

He grinned at her. All he knew was this moment, this second. Right now was all that counted. Because he didn't know what the hell was going to happen tonight.

TWENTY-SEVEN

Nia insisted that Rob go home to pick up anything he needed. He'd only be gone for a short time, and she could take care of herself. She didn't need a bodyguard.

Beside her, Bast snarled in a way that made Rob laugh and say even he understood that. "Just don't let anyone in," he added.

She nodded, but he made her promise, which she did immediately. She'd watched enough TV shows to know that letting anyone in was one sure way to end up bleeding on the floor.

And what would happen to Bast if she died first? Nia suspected there weren't many people around who understood a cat when the small animal scolded the human for not petting her in just the right spot.

"I'll be back in ten minutes." Rob frowned, and she knew he was mad at himself that he'd only told his brother to bring coffee and not a change of clothes.

But with Nia's promise, he jumped into his car and drove away.

Two minutes later, the doorbell rang, and Nia peered through the peephole at Debbie, whose appearance on her doorstep yesterday had started all the trouble.

Debbie looked different today. Not just from yesterday morning, she looked different from every time Nia had seen her since she'd come to the village. Debbie's shoulders, usually squared, were hunched. Her chin and lips, usually belligerent, were curved down.

She even looked thinner from yesterday. Like an inflated balloon that had lost its air.

Defeated. Sorry. Like a dog who'd done something wrong and was ready to grovel.

Unaware of Nia's gaze through the peephole, Debbie rang the doorbell again.

Nia stepped back and reached for the door handle. She could stay inside the house and talk to Debbie on the porch with the screen door between them. That wouldn't be dangerous.

The door creaked open. Instead of making Nia nervous or want to close the door again, the squeaking sound inexplicitly made her want to laugh.

What was she turning into?

Nia's reaction to Debbie shocked her more than her lovemaking last night with Rob.

Her urge to laugh caught in her throat.

"May I come in?" Debbie squinted at her on the porch side of the screen. Even her voice was different. Subdued. As if it had lost a few pounds, too.

"You can talk to me on the porch."

"Jerry called me."

Nia sucked in her lower lip and nodded. As if she had a hand in anything Jerry did, when she hardly knew him. The most she knew about Jerry was that Rob loved him – though she still didn't understand why Rob had come to her house instead of Jerry.

But she wasn't complaining. Maybe that was part of the miracle that brought Rob into her life.

"I'm sorry," Debbie said. "I'm so sorry. I told Justine that coming here yesterday wasn't a good idea. I didn't know anything about the gun."

Nia nodded. She believed Debbie. But she still wasn't inviting Debbie into her house. Believing someone and forgiving her was one thing. Nia had too much to live for now to take a chance that she was wrong about Debbie. Unlikely as it seemed, maybe Debbie was the one who tried to run her over.

Though the air outside was mild – probably just about perfect – Nia's skin chilled. It was a question that might never go away. She might look at people for the rest of her life and wonder *Are you the one? The person who ran me over?*

"Jerry thought you might like to know something about your brother." Debbie slipped her hand inside her purse. "He said you don't remember him or the rest of your family."

Nia tensed and clutched the door handle. Ready to slam it shut, then dive sideways to the floor. Out of the way of any bullets that might come through the thick wooden door.

Debbie pulled out a manila envelope. "I was in Eau Claire two years ago. I called Marc's house, and his wife invited me to a birthday party for their oldest son. I thought you might want to see the pictures."

Oldest son? Nia's thoughts seemed to have stopped, and she operated on a gut feeling that was screaming at her to look at the photos. She grabbed the screen door handle, turned it, opened it. Never taking her gaze from the envelope.

"Come in," she said.

Bast hissed behind her. Nia snapped to awareness, to suspicion. What had she done?

But Debbie was stepping inside already, blinking and smiling and looking gratified. For the first time not looking as if she wanted to wipe her feet on Nia's back.

It was too late to push Debbie out. Besides that, Nia's instincts were telling her that it was okay. That Debbie wouldn't hurt her.

And if Debbie did try to hurt her, Bast would move faster than Debbie and scratch her eyes out.

Rob's heart thundered as he pulled into Nia's driveway. He recognized the blue Chevy that Debbie had been driving since his second tour in Afghanistan, when she still worked at the cheese factory. He clutched the steering wheel, and his hands sweated, even as he remembered Debbie had been different back then without the expectation of inheriting money from Miriam. She dated the manager of a bowling alley in Tomahawk, and she used to drink at the bar and embarrass her daughter, who Rob heard lived in Dallas now with the husband that she'd met when they reached their goal weight the same day at Weight Watchers Online.

He slammed his foot on the brake. He didn't know what had changed Debbie, but figured it was money. Money did that to people.

For him, it was war.

For Nia, it was getting run over twice. Another life changer. Life and death. And it wasn't over with yet.

He punched his car into park. His heart raced like a train on a country track with no highway crossings for miles. Leaving the key in his Chevy, Rob jumped out and ran to the back door.

It was locked and he shook it uselessly. As if he could break it off, the urgency driving him. Stupid, stupid, stupid.

His teeth clenched, and he didn't know who he was

calling stupid, him or her.

He turned to leave for the front when the door opened and Nia stuck her head out. Her complexion seemed to be a shade lighter than normal but that could've been the light, with clouds drifting in the sky, filtering the sun. Like a scratched lens over a camera.

"Hey," she said.

He stared at her, his heart pounding, his body shaking. His mind shattering. "You're okay?"

"Uh-huh. Debbie's here. She has pictures of my brother and his family."

He walked to the back door as if he were normal. As if his heart still wasn't thumping crazily. As if he hadn't been that scared since the bomb went off in Afghanistan and he temporarily lost his hearing while he smelled smoke and burning flesh, afraid to turn his head in either direction.

When he entered the house, he saw Debbie was sitting at the kitchen table, looking like she'd settled down for a long gossip. Even smiling at him.

Something in his face must've changed her attitude. Made her think of the overdose and the trouble. Her lips twitched into a bad imitation of a smile and she got up, wincing a bit. He remembered she had arthritis, the reason she quit her job at the cheese factory, though she was too young to collect full social security.

"I'd better go home," she said.

He crossed his arms. Debbie didn't look dangerous, but the last time she was here, she'd brought along Nia's enemy.

Rob had learned in Afghanistan not to trust the natives. Wisconsinites were no better. Not even in this tiny village with its prophesy of a miracle that was probably a stunt pulled off by a local teen. Some kid who hoped it would picked up by the news stations. Only then would he pop up and say, "Me! Me! I did it. Look at me."

In the end, everyone was all for one – when the *one* meant the person in the mirror.

Debbie gave Nia a nervous smile. "You can keep the pictures. I don't need them."

"I can make copies and—"

Putting her hand out like a traffic cop, Debbie stopped her. "Don't bother. I'll just put them in a box and not look at them again. They're your family, not mine. You keep them."

It took a couple minutes before Debbie left the house and Nia sat at the table again, peering at the photos, a line creasing her forehead.

Rob leaned over the table. "What the hell were you doing?" He heard the suppressed anger in his voice and saw her wince, but he kept going. "Debbie not only brought your unhinged sister here, but afterward she overdosed Justine and put her in the hospital. She's the last person we need in the house."

Nia looked up at him. Not saying anything. But he felt her recoil. The way she kept her gaze from him. As if he were the one harming her.

He uncrossed his arms, sank onto the chair next to hers, then lowered his head to look her in her eyes. "Seeing her here, thinking of what could've happened, I was more frightened than I've been in my life."

She didn't blink. Didn't talk. But he felt her disappointment.

Normally he wouldn't defend his actions or his words. Normally he didn't give a damn.

Today he cared. Today he gave a damn.

"The worst part was knowing I wasn't here to protect you."

Nia's eyebrows rose. "I had Bast."

"She's a *cat*."

Bast meowed loudly and leapt onto the table, her four paws making a loud thump. Rob sat back and waited to see what she would do next. It was getting easier to believe Bast understood what he was saying.

She pranced up to him, put her face an inch from his, and said, "Yeow!"

Then she hissed. Turned her tail on him and padded away as if he were so beneath her he wasn't even worth her disdain.

He turned to Nia. "Did she just give me the cat version of the finger?"

Nia gave a spurt of laughter. "So, you are learning to speak Cat."

"A deaf person would've understood that."

Her smile dipped and she looked down at the photos. "Debbie was in Eau Claire two years ago." Nia's voice was low, the laughter gone. "She was at a birthday party for my brother's oldest son, Joey. He was just two then." She picked out a photo of a grinning toddler with what looked like spaghetti stains around his lips. She slid it in front of him. "The other boy was a baby. Debbie thinks he's two now."

The next photo pushed in front of Rob was of a plumpish, smiling woman with a baby.

"That's the baby's mom. My brother's wife. She looks...happy."

He nodded as another photo slid his way of a tall, handsome man. Like Nia's dad, but better looking, with a thinner face and serious eyes. Watchful eyes, Rob thought. But maybe it was the way the sunlight hit his eyes.

"What do you think?" she asked.

"He doesn't look like you." He shoved the photo away. "What else did she say?"

"Not much. Debbie said she hardly knows Marc. She was at a bowling tournament and saw a sign for his construction business in front of someone's house. She said she had a feeling it might be her cousin's boy. She called, the wife answered and invited her."

"They must've talked at the party."

"She said he didn't talk much, but he seemed like a nice guy. He's a Big Brother to inner city kids. The boy who was his little brother was there with his mother, and they were having fun."

"What else did she say?"

Nia shrugged one shoulder. "Debbie mostly remembered the food."

Rob nodded. That was the Debbie he knew.

"And the son's name." Her voice was hushed. "Harry. Debbie asked Marc's wife if the name ran in her family, and she said Marc was a Harry Potter fan."

"It looks..." Rob was going to say *suspicious*, but the half smile on Nia's face stopped him. "Auspicious. What else did she have?" he asked again.

Nia blinked and her forehead puckered. "She apologized to me. Maybe you'll want to know about that." The lines on her forehead deepened. "She hasn't told anyone yet, but she and her boyfriend are starting a website for bowlers. She's glad now that she didn't inherit the house. If she did, her boyfriend would never have suggested it. She really wants to do it. I think she loves him."

Rob nodded and wondered if he knew something Linda Wegner didn't know.

Maybe a miracle did just happen in the village of Miracle.

Then he looked into Nia's pensive face, put his hands on either side, leaned forward, and kissed her.

Her lips were soft beneath his. Pliant. Her skin soft and warm.

This was his miracle. *Nia.*

Now all they had to do was survive to enjoy this thing that was happening between them.

He pulled back, letting go of her face. "Do you really need to talk to your family yourself? In person?"

She sat back, putting distance between herself and his words. The rejection so clear on her face and her posture it could've been written on her forehead with a thick black marker.

"Forget it," he said. "It's a bad idea."

"The why did you say it?" Her voice was constrained and she looked away from him, her gaze landing on the photos. Hurt flashed across her face and then was gone.

"Your family doesn't deserve you. Someone should have seen what went on. I don't know who it was, but there were four other people in the family. Someone had to have known."

"My brother knows." She peered back at him, her eyes dull. The lips that had been soft under his a short time ago were pressed into a thin line.

"One other person knows," he said. "The would-be murderer."

"It's better to find out now, isn't it?"

"How likely is it that the person who did it will admit to it?"

Her shoulders lifted in an infinitesimal shrug. "You said someone will know. That's why I need to go."

He pushed his hand through his hair. This was getting worse and worse. He was really screwing this up. "Okay, we'll go. But you don't have to confront them. You can stay someplace where they won't recognize you."

Her mouth gaped open and she stared at him. "You're afraid for me. That's it, isn't it?"

"I'm scared as hell." He stared into her eyes. "I don't want anything to happen to you."

Her lips curved up in a smile that managed to look sad. Then she reached up and put her hand on the side of his head. "I don't want anything to happen to me, either. But I need to find this out. I need to face them."

"Once we face them, it's like sticking a spoon into a dirty pot. Either the dirt will swirl around and thicken. Or someone will finally kick the pot over and the dirt will run out." He leaned in closer to her. "When someone starts kicking, I don't want you to be the target."

She stared into his eyes as if she wanted to see into his soul. "What if I told you that I don't want *you* to be the target?"

He opened his mouth to tell her that her family didn't scare him, but she slid her hand from the side of his face over his mouth.

"Don't answer," she said. "You're not backing down, are you?"

He shook his head.

She lowered her hand. "Neither am I. I'm going. I don't want to do it, but I need to do it. I don't even need to know what happened earlier in my life. I just need to know that they'll leave me alone and will never come back and harm me." She looked at him fiercely. "If I face them, they'll know I'm strong and they'll stay away."

He didn't reply right away. He could hear the refrigerator motor click in. Outside a bird cawed. A crow. As if it had spotted a dead animal and was calling the other vultures. Letting them know dinner was ready.

"Your mind is made up?"

"My mind won't budge."

He stared and her, and she stared right back. He smiled slowly. "I wish you'd stay, but I'm proud of you for going."

"That doesn't even make sense."

"Life doesn't make sense. Anyway, Jerry will be there tonight. He won't let anyone hurt you."

"I'm not counting on Jerry." Her lips curved slightly, but her eyes...they bled sadness. "I'm counting on you."

He leaned forward, just a few inches, and kissed her. Only his lips touching hers. Making her a wordless promise that if anyone tried to kill her, they'd have to go through him to do it.

TWENTY-EIGHT

Nia felt calm in the passenger seat of Rob's car as they drove to the resort on the lake where her family was staying. Not calm like floating on Lake Miracle on a windless summer day, but a calm in the middle of a hurricane.

Her family.

Even the words sounded strange. As if she were about to eat a dish of something – like vanilla ice cream – that every other person was familiar with, but to her it was new. Exotic. Or the way she felt when she found out that the color blue was the same color as the sky and the water. A moment of wonder. Of discovery.

Of fright.

Her heart was beating fast. Not so calm after all.

As Rob pulled into the hotel parking lot, she glanced down at her lap and saw her hands were curled tightly on her thighs, the calm disappearing by the second.

Unclenching her hands, she inhaled deeply. The parking lot overlooked Lake Nokomis, about twice as wide and long as Miracle Lake. She should have felt calmed by that, too, but her tension rose as she left the car and turned toward the lodge. Eager to face her family and finish this, then go back to her house.

Back to her cat.

Back to her life.

At the lodge's registration desk, Rob told the middle-aged clerk with bright red hair and matching lipstick that they were waiting for the Beaudines. "Oh, number six," the clerk said. "They're in. They just called ten minutes ago and asked about a place to eat for dinner."

Rob said they were waiting for another friend. Nia watched the clerk closely to see if any suspicion sharpened her face. But the clerk just smiled pleasantly, her eyes blank. Probably thinking of her own life and her own problems.

Everyone had problems, Nia knew. Hers just seemed out of the ordinary.

Rob steered Nia into the lounge area with walls paneled in wood that went all the way up to a soaring ceiling. On the floor was a blue carpet. Nia decided she liked the paneling and the rug in the lodge, but not in her house.

She didn't know what she wanted in her house yet, which is why she hadn't bought new furniture.

Except Rob, she thought as they sat on a brown couch. She liked Rob in her house. And Bast, of course. But Bast would look good anywhere.

And Rob...

He would look best in the bedroom.

Naked.

She smiled at her secret thought and the picture it aroused in her mind. The tightness coiling inside her melted. Her pulse steadied. Her breathing became deeper and slower.

That's what happiness did, she thought. Even for a fleeting moment. It was like ice cream – which she seemed to be hungry for, with her mind going back to it again. Eating ice cream was...fabulous. But then it was gone. And soon she knew she would crave more.

That's the way she craved Rob.

In the parking lot, there had been about a dozen cars, but she, Rob, and the desk clerk were the only people in the lodge, the others probably on the lake or hiking or in their rooms. Nia turned her head. Out of the long windows facing the lake, she counted only three small boats on the expanse of blue water.

Maybe it wasn't the right time for fishing, but she didn't care enough to ask about it. Besides, it was a weekday and spring yet, with the weather changing by the minute. It was already getting a bit chilly and the sun had only started to lower in the sky.

She felt warm now. Too warm. And her stomach fluttered. They'd driven here ahead of Jerry, who'd been called to handle a disturbance and told them to go ahead and he'd be there soon. After they talked to her family, Jerry wanted to take her and Rob to dinner at a Chinese place in Tomahawk.

Right now she didn't think she could eat. The thought of food made her stomach clench.

"The lake is pretty," she said to stop the thoughts twirling in her head before they moved on to all the things that might go wrong.

"Jerry and I used to fish here with my dad when we were kids."

She looked at him. "You never talk about your dad."

"My dad was a drunk."

"Oh." She didn't know what else to say. "I'm sorry."

He shrugged. "It's okay now. He's been clean for four years. My mom divorced him when Jerry and I were sixteen. She works at the cheese factory and lives with her mom and dad at the farm. They're not doing so well, but they're independent as hell." He flashed her a grin, and her breath caught. In the short day and a half since she'd met him, he'd changed. He was smiling more. He seemed...almost healed. Almost happy.

"Your mom is like you," she said.

"And you." The smile remained on his lips but his eyes were serious.

Her heart beat fast, but not because of fear. Far from it. The warm feeling simmered inside her again.

"My mom pretends her parents are doing her a favor letting her stay with them," Rob said. "Grandma believes it, but I'm not sure about Grandpa."

"What about your father. Is he—"

"Cussing himself for losing a good thing? Trying to get her back?" His eyebrow arched. "Yeah, all that."

"It was tough, huh?"

He gave her a smile that made her catch her breath and think he was going to kiss her. Right now. In public.

It was the kind of smile the leading actor in a movie gave the leading actress. Before Nia met Rob, she didn't understood what the big deal was and thought her sex brain cells had been destroyed, too.

Now she knew those cells had been dormant. Sleeping. She'd just needed the right man to wake them up and activate them again.

They were activated right now. Wanting her to make up for lost time.

"Afghanistan was tougher," he said. "But in a lot of ways, your life was worse. What happened after the accident..." He paused, his smile gone, his lips a grim line. "And what happened before."

"I don't remember it, so it doesn't matter."

His face tightened and changed, turning from grim to dangerous. Like a cat shifting into a tiger. "They harmed you. It mattered."

"I can't let it matter." She put a hand to her throat, feeling her pulse throb beneath her fingertips. "Dr.

Whitcomb is right. I'm a new person. It would've been nice if my family had turned out to be wonderful people who loved me and cared for me." An ache thumped in her throat, and she ignored it. "But no matter what happened in the past, I have to go on. I'm not here for revenge or retribution. I just want them to leave me alone."

He just looked at her, his lips pressed together, and she could see he was holding back words.

Just as she held words back. Words like *I've got you now. I don't need them.*

She knew enough from watching TV not to say *those* words. It was too soon. Maybe it would always be too soon.

Until it became too late.

His eyes darkened, the air between them charged. Not too late now, she thought. Then her thoughts slowed even as her heart beat faster. Rob bent his head toward her, his lips parting. Her nostrils flared, she inhaled his scent. The musk stronger. Sending out a silent message.

He was going to kiss her.

She lifted her head to meet his—

The first notes of "Real Good Man" sang out from his cell phone.

They both jumped back. He grinned at her and she beamed back at him, a little breathless, her emotions changing by the heartbeat. As if she were on a twisting, turning amusement ride. A ride she couldn't remember taking and didn't think she wanted to.

But if the rides were as fun as the way she felt when she was in bed with Rob...then she wanted to leave right now, find an amusement park, buy a purse full of tickets, and go on it. Over and over and over.

Though engrossed in her thoughts, she still heard

Jerry telling Rob he was delayed. He was driving to another call, but it didn't look like it was anything big. Someone complaining his neighbors were too noisy. Jerry should be on his way to the lake soon, and Rob should keep her out of their way until he got there.

Rob slid a sideways gaze at her. "Nia doesn't like to be told what to do. I'll have to consult her about this."

While Jerry swore and called him a name, Nia laughed softly because Rob was grinning with a spark in his eyes.

He hung up, and a warm feeling wrapped around her heart, despite what was going to happen soon. As if they were a couple, Rob put his arm around her shoulders. Her eyes closed, she slowly leaned against him until her head rested against his shoulder.

She breathed his scent in again, this time deep into her belly. She felt so...good. Not as blissfully good as after sex with him, but quietly good. Sitting-in-front-of-the-fireplace good.

It wouldn't last long, and she determined to enjoy it while she had it.

The notes from "Real Good Man" rang again. Nia jerked away from Rob, as if she'd been caught doing something against the law.

"Yeah," Rob said into the phone.

Nia heard Jerry tell Rob there was a fight at the bar over a game of pool. Someone named Tommy was bleeding badly and he didn't know when he'd get there. He went on to say he'd heard from Debbie. Justine had checked out of the hospital. The family had planned to stay overnight at the lodge, but now that Justine was checked out, they decided to pack and leave early.

"I thought I'd catch them before they left," Jerry said, "but I might not make it."

Rob swore.

"Sorry, but work calls. I can hear the ambulance. I'll talk later."

Then he stopped talking and Rob closed up the cell phone and put it in his pocket before turning to Nia.

"You heard?"

"It looks like it's not going to happen," he said. "At least we know they're leaving."

She frowned. They were leaving, but what if one of them decided to come back?

Her palms turned sweaty. She didn't like this. Didn't like it at all.

TWENTY-NINE

It wasn't over until it was over, and Rob could tell this was as far from being done as a bloody steak on the grill. By Nia's scowl and frowning eyebrows, he could see she felt the same way.

"We can watch them," she said. "We can stand outside their door and I can listen to what they say."

"Is that what you want to do? Creep around their hotel room?"

She stood and narrowed her eyes at him, giving him a disdainful look that reminded him of Bast. "I know what creep means. It's sneaking around. I don't want to sneak. I didn't do anything wrong. Maybe I did before, but not this time."

He got to his feet. "We could just go home."

As he said *home*, he felt a shock because he was thinking of her home, not Jerry's.

It was too soon to feel that her home was his. But even as he told himself to slow down, denial reared up inside him. His heart saying it wasn't early. That love came like a speedball to some, and to others it was a long season filled with hits and misses and a hell of a lot of fouls.

He'd known her for less than two days, but he felt like he'd won the game already.

"I'm not ready to go home. I want to…" Her voice trailed off and her forehead crinkled. "You're looking at me like..."

"Like what?"

"Like you want to kiss me." Her voice was hushed.

"I always want to kiss you."

Her eyes wide, she gave a quick laugh, sounding surprised. Sounding...happy.

He felt the same way. In the midst of confusion and plans falling apart, *this* was happening.

It was like seeing a double rainbow between storms.

Nia was his double rainbow.

He bent his head and kissed her. A meeting of their lips. He had the feeling their hearts had already had their own meeting. Made their own secret pact.

When he pulled back, she gave a laugh that sounded breathless.

Good. She took his breath away, too.

"So, what are we going to do?" he asked. "There's no shame in leaving."

The laughter left her face. "There's no peace, either."

"It's your life. I won't try to stop you again. Whatever you decide, I'm with you."

She sucked in her breath. "I think I should confront them."

"*We* should confront them," he said, and his pulse only speeded a little. "The clerk said number six, right?"

Her shoulders squared, she nodded. "Let's get sixed."

He held his hand out. "Let's go get 'em."

She let him take her hand and they headed outside. The lodge had only twenty-six rooms, all the entrances on the outside, with the main lounge in the middle. Hand in hand, like high school kids, they strode toward number six, which wasn't far from where his car was parked.

They were nearing room three when a navy blue

pickup turned into the parking lot. As it angled into a spot two parking spaces from theirs, Rob spotted a company name painted in white on the side of the truck: Marc Beaudine Contraction.

He stopped walking.

In his periphery, Nia glanced at him. He felt her puzzlement, but he kept his gaze on the truck as a tall man got out. His short hair was sandy colored. He turned toward the sidewalk, the set of his lips grim.

Nia gasped. "It's Marc." She pitched her voice low. "He came after all. I wonder why."

Rob nodded. He wondered, too.

Was he friend?

Or enemy?

Marc's gaze glanced past then...and then back to them. Landing on Nia.

From his scowl, Rob guessed the answer wasn't *friend*.

Before he could say anything, Nia stepped in front of Marc, her spine determinedly straight, her head determinedly held high. "I'm Nia," she said, her voice purposeful. "You must be my brother Marc."

THIRTY

Emotion flashed across Marc's face too fast for Nia to read. Not that she was good at reading emotion. That's why she listened to what people said and, more importantly, the way they said it. Sometimes that's how she found out what they really meant.

The way their voices stumbled. The pitch of their voices, with laughter or sadness or anger. And even the way they paused – like Dr. Whitcomb did when he was trying to answer something and she knew he didn't really know the answer but didn't want to admit it.

Marc must've been smarter than Dr. Whitcomb. He nodded. His expression changed slightly, turning more stolid, as if he put on a mask that hid his eyes, nose, and lips. Nothing from the inside showed, his emotion hidden.

She wondered if that's how she looked to other people. As if she were holding her emotions inside and locked away.

Then Rob stepped to her side, not holding her hand anymore but close enough for her to feel his warmth. Like the sun's rays, but better. His nearness gave her strength and confidence.

She wasn't alone anymore. Someone besides Bast cared what happened to her.

It was hard to believe that yesterday morning when

she woke up, she didn't know Rob. Now it felt as if she'd known him forever. That if they hadn't met, there would've been something wrong with the world.

She didn't feel the same thing about her brother. She looked at Marc and felt no spark of recognition. It didn't matter that she'd heard his voice or she'd seen his picture. It didn't matter that she was sure he'd sent her books about Harry Potter, a character with the same name as his son.

She didn't feel a whisper of emotion. This man she'd been so eager to meet was nothing to her.

Looking at his expressionless face now, she felt heaviness in her heart. A sadness because deep inside her, she'd longed for a connection.

"Did you come to talk to the others?" she asked.

He stared a long moment. She couldn't read his face. She'd already established that being silent wouldn't force him to talk, but that was her only trick.

Raised voices came from nearby room number six, but Marc didn't look and neither did Rob. Neither did she, though she guessed they didn't hear the voices.

Marc finally nodded at her, as if he were reluctantly giving away government secrets.

She kept her gaze on him. He was a couple inches taller than Rob, over six feet with a muscular body. Rob had muscles, too. Just not ones like Marc's biceps that stood out below the sleeves of his black T-shirt without him flexing them.

From her quick up-and-down glance, she saw he didn't job out all his work. The left leg of his jeans above the knee was splashed with white paint. His work boots looked like he didn't watch where he stepped. His haircut was ragged. There were deep brackets around his lips for a man who was only twenty-nine, and he wore a silver band on his left hand ring finger.

So he'd left his wife home and two sons and had driven over two hours to Tomahawk to see the family. Not her. The *rest* of the family. She'd been a surprise. From his grim expression, she wasn't a pleasant one.

"I'm going with you," she said.

She felt Rob's apprehension. His worry that she was going to get hurt. His concern settled over her like Harry Potter's Cloak of Invisibility.

She firmed her chin. Getting hurt was part of being alive. If she continued to hold herself back while she observed other people and the things they did, she would never really live.

Marc nodded in the direction of room six. "It's not going to be pretty. Our family is a tough crowd. Are you strong enough to take it?"

"I can be tough." She blindly reached to the side for Rob's hand. His fingers clasped hers. "A car ran over me twice, trying to kill me. I lost all my memories, but I'm still alive. I think that makes me tougher than most people."

The left side of Marc's lip kicked up but it wasn't a happy smile. Not with the rest of his face unbearably sad. "You asked for it. If the wild animals attack, don't blame me."

His lips straightened and he headed toward room number six.

As Nia followed him, it occurred to her that though he hadn't shown any affection, he didn't seem to hate her.

Her eyes smarted and her stomach tightened with a rush of gratitude and relief. Accompanied by a powerful urge to cry. She gripped Rob's hand as tightly, and he squeezed hers back.

She told herself that in a minute or two, she would be

with her family and she needed to damp down all those emotions. To go back to being an observer for a short time.

But going back was hard. For this last day and a half she'd been *living* life, not just watching it. And some very bad things had happened.

And some very, very good things.

Marc took an extra long step and his knock on the door sounded as if the Norse god Thor had thudded his hammer against it.

The voices inside stopped.

"Who's there?" a man asked.

"Marc."

"Marc!" a woman said, her voice lilting with joy.

Nia's heart beat faster. That had to be her mother. The mother who didn't want to see her, Nia reminded herself. Brenda Beaudine didn't want to see her when she was in the hospital, and she certainly wouldn't want to see her now.

The door swung open. "May as well have a family powwow," a tall man said from inside the motel room. "The gang's all here."

Nia didn't know what he meant by gang, but she was a Beaudine, too. Sucking in her breath, she released Rob's hand and followed Marc in.

"Marc, thank God you're here," a woman said. "I missed you so—" She stopped, her mouth gaped open, staring behind him at Nia as if she were seeing a ghost.

Sounds exploded in the room, a woman screeched, a man yelled and another joined him as Nia stared at her mother, recognizing her from the photos on the computer. Brenda Beaudine stared back. Frozen. As if she didn't hear the noise swirling around her. As if they were the only two people in the room.

Ignoring the angry voices, Nia held herself still, her attention focused on Brenda, noting her green eyes, almost the same color as Justine's. Much brighter than Nia's gray-green.

And amidst all the noise, besides Marc and Rob, Brenda was the only one silent, staring at Nia with shock and something else...

Longing?

A shiver went through Nia. Then another and another. It was too cold in here. Then too hot. Her body flushed and she felt dizzy. Sick.

An arm slid around her shoulders. Rob.

Her breath stuttered and she reached behind his back and grasped a handful of his shirt. On the edge of hyperventilation, she sucked in a deep breath, then held it in before she released it in a slow exhale.

Her body calmed slightly, her senses settled. The ranting from the two men finally got through to her. The younger man was calling her a bitch and a liar, and he ordered her to leave. Justine's husband, she thought. Andy. The older man's face turned red as he asked Marc why the hell he brought *her*.

She knew him from his pictures on his real estate website. Her father who hated her.

Justine sat on the side of the bed, as if her legs wouldn't hold her. She held her cupped hands over her mouth. She looked paler and thinner than when Nia had last seen her outside her front door. More like a weak kitten than a tigress about to attack. On the bed were two open suitcases half filled. They'd been packing.

Nia's gaze whipped back to her father, the man making the most noise. Spewing anger and hate. His photos on the website hadn't been airbrushed too much. Maybe some extra flesh around the jowls and waistline.

Though he could afford to lose twenty pounds or so, he was a handsome man. And with his height, he carried the weight well.

Except for her, the whole family was tall. All of them with hair in shades of golden brown hair and olive coloring.

Nia imagined that as a child, she must have felt unlike them. Like the runty, spotted puppy when the rest were all tall and golden.

But if they loved her and treated her like one of them, that wouldn't have mattered, would it?

Unless she was evil right from the start. On TV, Nia had seen children who were born with something wrong in their heads. Maybe she'd been one of those children.

But the mean and ugly part of her brain had been crushed under the tonnage of a car. She wasn't that person anymore.

All these thoughts whirled around her head in seconds and she wondered why she felt nothing as she stared at her father. She could look at the mail lady who dropped off infrequent bills and feel more reaction. In a distant way, she liked the mail lady. She would even worry slightly if she heard the mail lady were sick.

But this man... The longer she looked at him, the more she didn't like this man with his face mottled with anger and hate.

Shifting his gaze to Marc, her father pointed at her. "I want her out of here." Each word shot out like a bomb aimed at her, meant to hurt and maim.

Rob drew his arm from her waist and stepped forward.

Nia reached out, clasped his arm, and tugged him back to her side. With him next to her, she felt strong enough to face the family. She didn't need him to protect her. She just needed him to be here for her.

"My sister is staying," Marc said. "It's time she learned the truth."

THIRTY-ONE

With Marc's words, a silence fell. But anger simmered in the room. Boiling over. Ready to splash out and leave burn scars.

To Nia the silence was worse than the angry words. It almost felt as if she were used to yelling instead of silence. But that wasn't right. The opposite was true.

For now, at least. But maybe before Nia's brain damage, when she lived with these people...

Her breath shuddered, and she drew her breath in. Made it shallow, almost silent.

She must not let anyone hear. She must not show her fear.

The thoughts and reaction came out of nowhere, shocking her.

Next to her, Rob nodded at Marc. "What the hell is the truth you want to reveal?"

There was a gasp and Nia realized it came from her. *Shut up. Shut the hell up.*

Don't let him see you're scared.

She closed her mouth and became still. Silencing the voice in her head that was strident with dread.

She needed to concentrate. To find out why everyone hated her.

Marc turned to her. "You tell them."

Fear fluttered inside her chest and she stared at him.

"What you told me on the phone," he said. "About the

PTSD."

She opened her mouth and nothing came out. Just a croak. She tried again and this time it was worse. She looked up at Rob and put her hand over her throat, her pulse racing beneath her cold fingers.

Rob's brown eyes warmed with acceptance and understanding. And it could've been her imagination, but there was something more. Something that glowed in his eyes and seemed to come from his heart.

She still shook and she still felt sick, but she forced her lips into a smile. Making the effort for him.

"You figured out what was wrong." Her voice rasped, but she continued. Something inside her told her to go on. Told her not to cower, or *he*, her father, would win. "You should tell it."

She wasn't afraid to talk to the others. Not anymore. But she could see Rob *wanted* to do something for her. He couldn't shoot them or beat anyone up like men did on TV. That would just get him arrested. And she thought that maybe he would be okay with that.

In some way she couldn't understand, it would validate him...

But *this*...standing up to her family for her...this he could do and no one would arrest him. And it would be something that would make him feel better.

He gave her a half smile, as if he knew she was doing this for his ego, then his lips straightened and he faced her family. His gaze clear, he spoke in his clear tenor voice that commanded attention. "I was in Afghanistan for four tours. I know a lot about PTSD. You need me to spell it out?"

They shook their heads, and something in the room altered. Nia inhaled, sniffing the air but unable to smell anything except perfumes and maybe anxiety.

"Most people think it only happens in war," he continued, "but for some people – abused people – life is like a war zone." He looked from one to another and when he spoke again, his voice was as hard as a slap on the face. "Especially when it happens to kids."

Nia hadn't thought the words said out loud would hurt like someone socked her in her throat. Her jaws clenched. And the shivers slammed back, harder. She crossed her arms, but that didn't stop the shudders.

At least she closed her mouth tight, keeping whimpers from creeping out of her throat.

And that's when she knew she'd been this way before in front of these people. She didn't remember what happened, she just knew this wasn't the first time. The details were gone, but not the emotion. Not the fear nor the horror nor the twisting in her belly and tightness in her throat.

She looked from one family member to another as Rob spoke about the letters and what they said and why he concluded there was abuse. Since her behavior started as a child, even a baby with her constant crying, he said the abuse probably happened early on.

The smell thickened, and she inhaled again. Fear and anger. No, not just anger. It was anger multiplied. Rage. A festering, horrible rage.

She looked at the faces. Marc's face contorted and he grabbed his hair on the back of his head so tightly it had to hurt. Her mother was shaking her head, her mouth slack with disbelief.

But in her eyes...a mix of fear and denial.

Still sitting on the bed, Justine shifted her gaze to the floor, her lips shaped in a pout.

Her husband put his arm around her. His lips turned down, and he looked like he wanted to throw up.

Only Nia's father remained stolid. Watching. His jaw set, his lips set. Not taking his gaze from Rob.

Nia rubbed her arms, small bumps on them. Not goose bumps. *Fear* bumps.

Her shaking increased. Harder. Faster. She felt like a bridge crumbling to pieces, about to collapse.

"I can see what's happening," her father said, his voice steel-hard. "You're falling for her. Just like Andy did." He shot Justine's husband a glance of disdain before turning the disdain back to Rob. "Nia will make a man do anything for her."

"Clark, please." Brenda frowned at him. "There might be some merit in what this man is saying. I should have had her tested when she was young. I wanted to but you always said that she was just spoiled and—"

"And you never questioned why?" Marc stepped toward their parents in the small room. His angry voice with the words bitten off bounced off the walls.

Brenda gasped. Justine still stared at the floor, her shoulders hunched. Nia's brother-in-law looked around wildly, then his gaze stopped on the wastebasket by the corner desk. As if he thought he might need it soon.

Rod put his hand on Nia's shoulder and she could feel his tension. Unable to control herself, she started to rock back and forth, her arms still crossed.

"Marc!" Clark shouted. "I don't know what you're getting at but—"

"The truth. That's what the hell I'm getting at." Marc stabbed his index finger toward Rob. "Everything he said is true. I was a kid when I figured out what he was doing." He gave a snarling glance at Clark. "It's been killing me for years."

"Nooooo." Justine put her hands over her mouth, her eyes wide, her legs backed against the bed. "Nooooo."

"The worst part was I never said anything. Even when I found out someone tried to kill Nia, I didn't say anything. Not to the police. Not to the doctor. Not to anyone."

"There was nothing to say," Clark shouted. "Nothing!"

Marc kept his gaze on his mother. "Didn't you ever wonder why I stopped talking to the family?"

"Your father told me you were…" Brenda stared at Clark, shaking her head, her complexion as pale as the sidewalk. Tiny wrinkles that Nia hadn't seen before showed around her eyes and lips.

She was aging in front of Nia. Aging years in seconds of real time.

"Lies!" Clark shouted. "Don't believe him. It's all lies."

"Yeah, that's right. It's never you, Dad. It's always Nia's fault." Marc spoke to him with contempt, his lips in a sneer. "Always someone else's."

He turned back to Brenda, who was staring from her son to her husband to Nia with horror. Her skin the color of white chalk. "C'mon, you knew." Marc's voice grated. His posture was rigid, the cords in his neck distended. "You must've known. I have a daughter now—"

"A granddaughter!" Brenda put her hands over her chest, as if he'd stabbed her in her heart. "You didn't tell me."

"You think I wanted *him* to know I had a daughter?" Marc's nostrils flared and he looked at Clark as if he were something a Great Dane had left steaming on the sidewalk. "She's six weeks old. I can't take the chance that he'd do to her what he did to my sister."

"She's not your sister! I had a vasectomy!"

Brenda cried out, her mouth open, repulsion on her face, as if she were looking at a monster.

Clark's lips pulled back from his large teeth. He stood

with his legs braced, his hands curled into fists, his face red. He glared at his wife as if he wanted to put his hands around her neck.

"I knew you wanted another baby, so I didn't tell you. Even when you got pregnant, I gave you the benefit of the doubt. I was a virile man and thought maybe it didn't take..." He stopped, his breaths huffing, as if he'd run a mile.

A small cry came from Brenda, but no one else said anything, the air thick with silent shock and repugnance.

Nia bent forward, her stomach tight, as if a serpent were coiled inside her.

Only the serpent wasn't inside her. It was outside, in the form of a man.

"But when I saw her," he went on, his voice like a fully loaded semi crunching over gravel, "the tiny newborn with her black hair, I knew whose baby it was. How fucking dumb do you think I am?"

"You never said anything," Brenda whispered, her eyes pooling with tears.

"And give you the excuse to leave me?" His nostrils flared. "I knew as long as I didn't rock the boat, you'd stay. Besides, you needed someone to stay home to take care of the kids while you worked all those nights on the supposed emergency calls."

"Oh God." She stepped back from him. "Oh God. So you abused her? Did you—" She stopped, her breaths rasping. "Did you—" She stopped again, and then a cry tore out of her that raised the hair on Nia's arms.

Brenda shook her head, her breaths gasping. When she spoke again, her voice trembled. "Was that some sick way of getting back at me? Ruining a child's life?"

"Don't blame me. If you hadn't cheated on me—"

Nia groaned. Sick with it all. Sick to her stomach and

her heart and her soul.

Clark shifted to look at her. "You were the cause of it all. You and your fucking—"

"Stop!" Rob roared out the command. They all turned to stare at him, instant silence in the room. "You're sick. You should be locked up. I should call the sheriff."

"You can't prove anything," Clark said. "Marc never saw anything. No one ever did." He shot Nia a look of hatred. "And *she* doesn't remember."

"I feel awful. Just awful." Brenda's hand was over her mouth. She lowered it and looked at Nia. "Can you forgive me?"

Nia couldn't answer. Her knees felt like they were made out of pudding. If not for Rob's arm around her shoulders, she didn't know if she could stand.

Brenda stepped toward her. Nia shook her head and held out her hands to ward off this stranger who happened to be her mother.

"Not today." Nia's voice rasped, and the words coming out of her throat hurt. But the shudders were dying down. The worst was over. She knew the truth now. They all did.

When she and Rob entered the motel room, the man who wasn't her father had been in the center of his family. Now he stood apart, his hands fisted at his thighs, his breaths puffing out.

"I didn't know." Brenda lifted her hands in a pleading position. "I didn't have any idea."

"You want to know why?" Clark demanded, ugliness snaking in the air around him. Invisible but Nia felt it. "Because she was too busy fucking her boyfriend."

Brenda cried out, her hand to her face again, as if that would shut out what happened in the past, and the words that were said in the room. The truths and the hatred and the ugliness.

Nia wondered if a normal person would feel pity for her. But Nia felt too distanced. Too numb. Maybe if her mother had visited her in the hospital at least once...

"You didn't want to know," she said. "I don't think you cared enough about me."

Brenda looked wounded, her green eyes bruised, as if Nia had hit her.

"She didn't care for any of us." Justine's voice wobbled. "I'm sorry, too. I knew what Daddy was doing, but I pretended I didn't. Even to myself. And I didn't want to say anything because when he hurt you, he was nicer to me."

"Oh God," Brenda whispered. "Oh my God."

Justine's gaze stayed on Nia. "And you were so mean that I thought maybe you deserved it."

Nia's stomach heaved. She grasped Rob's arm and tugged. "I know what happened now. I don't want to stay any longer. Let's go home."

THIRTY-TWO

"I'm not leaving until I find out who ran you over."

Rob caught Nia's eyes. The only one in the room who mattered to him. If the others all died of a mysterious gas that killed everyone but him and Nia, he wouldn't feel a shred of pity.

"I just want to—"

"And then ran you over again," he continued, "and left you for dead. Left you in an alley as if you were a piece of garbage."

The mother gave another cry. He spared her a look, slicing his gaze over her horrified face.

You're too late to be horrified, lady, he thought viciously. Too fucking late.

He turned back to Nia. Not giving a damn about the rest of them.

"When I enlisted, I swore to support and defend my country." The silence in the room seethed around them as he continued. "I did it. My friends did it. And some of them died because of it."

Nia cried out softly and lifted her hand to his cheek. He raised his hand and held her palm against his skin. Watching the liquid pool in her eyes but not fall. Not one teardrop, like a brave soldier.

"Now I'm swearing to support and defend you," he went on. "If need be, I'll die defending you."

"You won't die," she whispered fiercely. "I won't let

that happen."

He smiled slowly. "Then let me do this. I want to make sure we both live for a long, long time."

Her smile wobbled at him. He released her hand and as if she understood what he had to do, she slid her hand from his cheek and stepped back.

Already missing her touch, he faced the roomful of people that included at least one would-be murderer.

"You can't pin what happened on me," Clark said. "I was showing a client a house."

"I was working that day at the clinic," Brenda said.

Clark's laugh sounded like acid splashing on metal. "With your clothes on or off?"

She turned on him. "Don't talk to me like that, you child molester. You pervert."

"Adulterer."

"Stop, stop. You're all disgusting." Tears ran down Justine's face. "I was trying on bridesmaids dresses with my friend Amy."

"I was at my brother's," the brother-in-law said.

"You think we were the only ones who hated her?" Clark gestured at Nia like she was garbage. Like she was nothing. "There's a whole line-up of people who hated her. You don't know the bitch she was before."

"But you do." Rob heard the rumble in his voice, and his hands clenched and unclenched. "You made her that way."

Clark's lips clamped together and he stared above Rob's head. Not looking sorry.

Not yet.

"Justine and I were both looking for leads that day." Justine's husband glared at Clark. "He was gone. Said he was showing a house and not to bother him unless it was an emergen—"

"Andy!" Justine clamped her hand on his arm. "Don't say anything more."

"Why?" Andy frowned at Justine. "I'm saying the truth. This is sick stuff. Really sick. I'm starting to feel sorry for Nia. I'm starting to see why she did some of the things she did."

"Her again." Justine gave a hard, sharp laugh that made Rob narrow his gaze. "It's always about her."

"You're sick, baby. The attention your father gave her wasn't right."

Justine frowned and looked away from him. Her hands lowered and she turned to Rob. "We were in the office all day. We have call logs. If you want them, I can get them to you."

Rob nodded shortly. "I want them." He wasn't taking anyone's word for it.

"We were operating that day." Brenda stared at him, her gaze unflinching. She looked ravaged but he couldn't feel any pity for her.

"You can prove that."

She nodded firmly. "Yes." She finally turned and speared Clark a look of scorn. "And you, Clark? Can you prove where you were?"

His mouth worked before he spoke, his face red. "I don't have to prove anything to him."

Hate surged up inside Rob. Hot and cold and murderous.

Marc stepped toward his father. "What about the police?" he demanded. "Can you prove it to them?"

Clark turned his sneer on his son. "What about you, Mr. Lily White? Can you prove what you were doing that day?"

"In a second. A good dozen people can swear that I was in Eau Claire all day."

"And he didn't have a reason to kill me." Nia spoke up, her voice clear even with a throb in it. "Of all of you, he was the only one who admitted knowing what happened."

"But I didn't stop it." Marc looked at her, and his expression was agonized, his lips twisted. "Maybe I had an excuse when I was a kid. But I'm an adult now. A dad. I should've said this after the accident, but I didn't."

Marc turned back to his father. "What you did to her. What we did to her." His hand swept the room, including his mother, his sister, his brother-in-law. "And what we didn't do. It's unforgivable."

"Yes." His mother stepped to his side and stared at her husband. "Unforgivable."

Marc glanced at her, his eyes dark and hard, and stepped away from her. She gave a cry of pain, but Marc didn't look at her again.

Rob watched them all. Alert. As if this were a war zone. Because that was sure the hell what it felt like.

"It's time to get this out in the open," Marc said.

"It's going to kill our business." Clark shook his head. "It's going to kill *your* business. You can't afford it."

Marc didn't flinch. Like a soldier who knew he was about to walk into death, he was ready for it. "It doesn't matter. Doing the right thing matters."

"Bullshit. It matters." Clark sent his wife a scathing look. "It's all I have." His lower jaw jutted out. He looked at Nia, and hate streamed from his pores. "She stole our clients. And once she was in the hospital, I got most of them back. We were saved."

Brenda gave a cry. "That's why you did it? Because of the business?"

"What the hell else did I have?" His gaze scorched her. "A slut for a wife?"

"You beast." Her voice was low with disgust. "You're sick, Clark. Sick."

He started back at Rob. "The police won't be able to prove I did anything. They couldn't last time, and they won't this time, either. But if this goes public, none of us will matter. You'll ruin the business."

"Last time we covered for you." Andy stood. "That's why the police didn't find anything. I'm not doing it this time."

"You're fired."

"Daddy!" Justine slowly rose to her feet.

"It's me and you." He held out his hand to her. "The way it should be. You're my real daughter. My blood. You won't turn on me like him. You'll stand up for me." His lips twisted into a grotesque imitation of a smile. "Won't you, baby?"

"I'm going to be sick." Justine put her hand over her mouth. Andy put his arm around her waist and pulled her to his side.

"We're going to be okay," he said. "We'll see a therapist. We'll get over this."

She leaned against him and nodded, her eyes moist.

A movement switched Rob's gaze back to Clark. His upper lip had lifted.

"I don't need you." He looked around the room, and if his eyes had lasers, they would all be writhing on the floor, dying. "I don't need any of you. I should've left you a long time ago."

Danger vibrated in the air. Rob bunched his muscles, ready to attack.

"I wish you had left me," Brenda said, her voice tortured, and her face seemed to age another decade. "I'm at fault for what I did, but what you did... It was evil."

"I hate you." Justine's voice was pitched high, and she sounded childlike. "I hope you go to jail for a long time. I never want to see you again."

"I won't go to jail." Clark poised on the balls of his feet with his hands curled into fists, reminding Marc of a fighter with nothing to lose. A fighter who would do anything to win. "I'll leave the state. Go where it's warm. I'll start over without all of you to hold me back."

"You're not going anywhere," Rob said, and Clark snapped around, his chest visibly pumping up and down. "It was you who did it." Rob's words came out solid, unfaltering. He knew what he said was true like he knew he was a twin and his mother loved him.

And so did Nia.

Not even two whole days, and she loved him and he loved her.

In the middle of this horror, he felt a rush of joy and strength.

"No one can prove I did anything," Clark said.

"I don't need proof. I know the truth here." Rob thumped his knuckles over his heart. "I'm not letting you walk away." He took a step toward him. "I know your kind. You blamed a child for all your bad luck last time. You'll blame her again. And to silence her, you'll do anything to shut her up for good."

"It *was* her fault."

"A baby?" Rob took another step. Only three feet from Clark now. "A child?"

Clark's face went ruddy, the color of a tomato. Sweat popped out on his forehead. "She wasn't my child, damn it. She deserved everything I did."

Rob took one last stride, his arm pulled back. Clark's eyes widened and he pulled his upper body back.

The movement was too late, Rob's fist coming at him

with the speed of anger. His knuckles plowed into Clark's left cheek and jaw. Bone against bone. The sound cracked in the air.

Clark's face jerked aside ninety degrees. Then almost leisurely, as if it happened in slow motion, he crumbled.

Rob's knuckles stinging, he watched Clark's legs collapse, his back bending forward. Nia ran to Rob's side and clutched his arm. He was aware of the others watching and not objecting. As if they were observers at a gladiator fight.

Making a choking sound, Clark finally thumped onto the thin motel rug.

Rob leaned forward, his hands in fists again. Nia released his sleeve. The others still didn't move, as if they were waiting for the next act.

But nothing happened. Clark still didn't move. Not even his chest. Or his open eyes that stared at Marc's shoes.

Unclenching his fists, Rob straightened.

"I think he's dead," Nia said. "I don't hear him breathing."

Stepping away from the body, Rob watched Marc go down to his knees and bend over his father. His mother the nurse stood as if frozen, watching, with her face blank.

Rob slid his arm around Nia while Marc felt for a pulse in Clark's throat. Seconds slipped by before Marc looked up and swept his gaze around the room. "He's dead."

"He had a small stroke last year." Justine spoke tonelessly, her gaze at her husband blank. "He didn't want anyone to know. I suppose he had another one."

No one moved or even spoke. They could've been a tableau in a wax museum.

Nia looked up at Rob. "Let's go home."

He nodded and turned to her, the energy draining from him. Home sounded right to him. Home with Nia.

THIRTY-THREE

Nia grabbed Rob's hand as they walked away from the others, her steps robotic. She wondered what she should feel, because right now she felt nothing for the dead man on the hotel room carpet.

She felt more pity for a dead spider.

As they reached the sidewalk, Nia heard footsteps behind them. She could tell by the heaviness of the step that it was her brother in his work boots.

Half brother.

Marc didn't say anything and neither did they. Their car was closer than his pickup. As they turned toward it, Marc called out Nia's name.

"Later on, maybe we can...talk?"

She looked at him for a long moment, glad that Rob was at her side. Dusk was coming down, the sky grayish. The same way she felt inside.

Then her emotions swooshed back. So much, it overwhelmed her. Tears burned her eyes, and she blinked them away. *I will not cry, I will not cry.* Her voice was fierce in her mind.

She saw Marc was blinking hard, and she wanted to ask him if he were about to cry, too. He rubbed the back of his knuckles against his nose. Then he stood with his chest out, his arms at his side, his brown leather boots braced on the drive.

"Yes," she said. "We can talk."

"I didn't protect you," he said, his voice rough. Though he still didn't speak, his eyes turned red.

Her eyes were probably red, too.

"You stood up for me." Her voice was thick and she pulled her hand from Rob's in case she needed to dig in her pocket for a tissue. "You were willing to hurt your business for me."

"He'll tell you." Marc nodded at Rob. "I should've done something long ago."

She stared into Marc's eyes that were the same shade of blue as the man's on the floor of room six. "I'm doing my life over. You can do yours over, too. We can do better this time."

He nodded. "I try. Every day I try."

They looked at each other for a long moment, but there didn't seem much to say. Or maybe there was too much to say, and neither of them knew how to say it.

"I'll call you." Nia took Rob's hand. He squeezed hers, and they headed toward his car.

Five minutes later, they were on the highway heading for Miracle.

"How're you doing?" Rob asked.

"I'm not sure. I'm kind of numb."

"How do you feel about...the dead man? You handling it okay?"

"He wasn't my real father. I don't remember him. I don't feel anything for him."

"I do." His voice was fierce. "I'm glad he's dead."

She looked at him. "I'm glad, too, but I'm mostly glad you didn't kill him."

From the twitch in his cheek, she thought he was sorry for it.

"He's not worth going to jail for." She put her hand on his arm, and it took a minute before the stiffness eased.

She released his arm and sat back. "But I'm sure Bast will be disappointed that we didn't kill anyone."

He laughed, and she grinned, too. She wondered if she should be laughing, but then she thought she should. After all, the dead man had hated her. He'd tried to kill her. His death was her freedom.

Though her freedom started before today. Eighteen months earlier.

"In the end," she said, "his trying to kill me was probably the best thing that happened to me. If that part of my brain hadn't been destroyed, I might never have gotten over what he did to me."

"I don't believe that." Rob looked at her. "But as long as you don't want me to stay away, I'm okay with that."

Emotion filled her, choking her so she was unable to talk. But she *felt*. Oh God, did she feel, the numbness gone. It was as if all the months of observing were a prelude leading up to this huge orchestra of emotion inside her, wanting to make music. Loud music. Joyous music. Music that would soar up to the heavens.

And it was good. The rising mix of wonder and sweetness and laughter and joy inside her shoved aside the hate and the jealousy and all the other ugly emotions that had roiled up, making her own poison.

But that poison was gone now, pushed out by the happy mix of emotions. Like the bright light of the sun pushing out the blackness of a moonless night.

"Let's go home." She paused a second, then continued, "So we can make love."

He stomped on the gas pedal. She leaned her head back and closed her eyes. Tears squeezed through and traveled down her face. But she wasn't crying for herself, she was crying for the girl she'd been before the accident. The poor, mixed-up girl.

The accident had changed her brain. She wasn't *that girl* any more. She was *this woman*.

Turning her head, she opened her eyes, the tears drying. After all that happened, she was the lucky one.

And this was just the beginning.

THIRTY-FOUR

All was right in the world.

For now.

Nia lay in bed, her mind at peace and her body...feeling good. Very, very good. Like a kid-at-Christmas good.

The curtains were pulled back and there was a full moon, the light filtering into their bedroom like watered-down sunlight.

Next to her, Rob lifted his arms and linked his fingers beneath his head, staring at the ceiling, his lips a line.

Her memories were wiped out, but she was sure this was not the desired expression of a man who'd just made a woman shout three times, scaring her cat out of the room – though she suspected Bast would argue that she hadn't been scared, just bored.

And at the end of their lovemaking, Rob had made a roaring sound. Like a crack of thunder just before the brilliance of the lightning.

She'd been hit by that lightning, too.

Not a bad way to end a day.

"I wish he'd been punished more," Rob said. "He got off too easily. It was practically painless. He just fell and was gone."

"It happened just as I wanted. *You* are my hero." She sat up, the cover slipping off her. And she didn't care. She sat cross-legged, exposing herself to him. And she didn't care. She didn't fear. "For the first time since I woke up in the hospital, I feel safe."

Rob frowned, and she could see he wasn't totally convinced. She blamed it on TV and the movies where the bad guy was beat up or killed in the end. Or in jail, though that wasn't as popular an ending.

Real life was different from TV. Even she knew that.

"All the secrets were revealed," she said. "The truths are out for everyone to see. None of them has any reason to try to kill me. They'll leave me alone. They have no choice."

She leaned toward him, touched his hair and felt the spring beneath her fingertips. Felt the life in him. And it wasn't just life. It was his life *force*.

He was a man that other men listened to. She'd felt it in the motel room. She'd felt it with Dr. Whitcomb. Rob was a man other men respected.

He was a man she loved with her whole heart.

Her sister coming to her house with the gun two days ago was the best thing that happened to Nia. It changed her life.

It was her miracle, like her cat talking.

"He should've had to pay for what he'd done to you. For making your life hell."

"A life I don't remember."

"But it *happened*." Rob's voice thickened with passion. "We need that for a happy ending."

Another rush of emotion filled Nia. Laughter and joy and a little sadness. She turned to the man on the bed beside her. "Don't you get it? *This* is the happy ending." She tilted forward, onto her knees, threw her arms around him and kissed him.

She'd been comparing life to what happened on TV, but this wasn't like anything on TV. It was better. More like a book, she thought. This book was over, and now she and Rob could start a new one. It would be their sequel. Or just Book Two, because she wanted to have many more with him.

But Rob was pulling back, and she saw his eyes glowing in the moonlight. "I wonder if this was part of the miracle," he said, repeating her thoughts. "All this and your talking cat, too."

"You believe in Bast?" A sense of wonder grew inside her. She felt...starstruck.

"I believe in you. For a long time I was walking around with a big empty hole inside me, but now that hole is healed." His brown eyes glowed brilliantly. "I'm happy."

"Me too." She laid her head on his chest, closed her eyes and listened to the strong beat of his heart beneath her ear. She stayed like that for a moment, and then a small weight sprang onto the bed.

Nia opened her eyes and saw Bast a foot away, kneading the cover as she did her pleasure dance.

She meowed twice.

"What's she saying?" Rob asked.

"She said 'me too.'" And Nia laughed and so did Rob, and Bast danced faster.

Miracle Pie
A Miracle Interrupted novel, book 4

Edie Ramer

Katie Guthrie has pie magic. *No special ingredients required...intuition tells her what to bake. Whether it's a Goodbye Pie or a Welcome Home Pie, it'll turn out perfect and be waiting for the person who needs it most.*

But when her best friend begs Katie to film a cooking show, there's no pie in the world that can help Katie out of her predicament—she'd never let a friend down, but she doesn't want to go in front of a camera. Especially when the man wielding it is the boy Katie left behind when she started her life over in Miracle, Wisconsin. The boy she used to call angel.

Gabe Robbins is no angel, and he's no boy anymore. *Burned out after a three-year stint building a hospital in Africa, Gabe ignores his demons by living day-to-day and filming wedding videos. Nothing deep, nothing he has to become invested in. Nothing that will get under his skin, until...*

Watching Katie create her pies from behind his video camera makes him realize what he's missing. He's put his life on hold for too long, wasted too much time. Thanks to Katie and her pies, Gabe discovers his passion again. But will it lead him to his heart's desire...or will this miracle take him away from Katie forever?

Excerpt:

Gabe bent over the keyboard. Mumbling that he didn't want to show the cooking part, he fast-forwarded to the end of the show. The video moved again at regular speed, showing her standing stood behind the counter. But he was the one talking on the video, asking, "Tell us, why pies? Why not cakes or cookies or cupcakes?"

He must have edited Rosa's objections out, because she was wrinkling her nose then leaning over the counter and saying, "Pies are love."

He laughed softly. "Tell me how pies can be love."

Sitting next to her tormentor while she watched the screen, Katie groaned and laughed and covered her eyes and then uncovered them. Finally, the video ended, freezing with her bemused face looking back at her.

"What do you think?" he asked.

"I don't know."

He twisted in the chair, so close she could see three shades of blue in his eyes. See that his eyelashes were golden brown, darker than his hair. Close enough that she could lean forward and kiss him.

She drew in her breath.

"I thought it was great," he said. "So did Taz. Viewers will love it."

"You mean..." She sat back in her chair and shook her head. Shaking the thought of kissing him right out of her mind.

"I can't promise it will go viral, but I can promise a lot of views. Not with just this one—we'd have to do a series of similar videos to build your viewers. We can do it.

You're passionate about pies. People love passion. They can get recipes anywhere, but what you have is unique. They'll love you. They'll want to watch you. They'll tell their friends about you."

She shook her head again. Sometimes she thought she might be a little insane, but she was nowhere near as insane as this man.

"I can't."

"You don't have to do anything. Leave it to me. I'll do it."

She shifted her gaze. Not toward the camera but toward the back door. Wishing she could step outside. The sun was out. Coming home this morning after delivering pies to the truck stop and the Italian restaurant in Tomahawk, she noticed a few yellow and orange leaves on the sugar maple tree in the front yard. In the dawn redness it looked like an old painting. She had an urge to go outside and see them now, in full sunlight.

"You're afraid," he said.

Her head snapped around. "No."

His eyebrows lifted. "It's very common. Some people are afraid of greatness."

"I bake pies." Her tone was sharp. What didn't this man understand about baking a pie? Anyone could do it. In fact, everyone *should* do it. If all the leaders of all the countries in the world went into their kitchens and made at least one pie every day, the world would no doubt be a better place.

Slowly, her breaths shallow, she turned her gaze back to him. He watched her. Unmoving. Implacable.

She wanted to kick him.

"I promised Rosa to do this with her. I can't do it with you."

"It's not the same thing. She's doing a show. What we're doing is small moments of time."

"You sound like a politician."

He put his hand over his heart. "You wound me."

"If the knife fits..."

Dropping his hand, he leaned closer again. Inches away. His blue eyes brilliant, enthralling her so she couldn't pull back or look away. "Think of the videos like movie trailers. If they become popular, it will make her show all the more valuable. In fact, I'll ask Rosa to do some."

"She said yesterday she doesn't want to do short videos."

"Then she doesn't have to. It will be just you and me."

"You're worse than a bulldog."

"I promise..." his smile returned... "I don't bite."

She gritted her teeth and put both hands to her hair, grabbing handfuls. *This man. This insane man. Couldn't he leave me in peace?*

"You have no excuses," he said.

"I don't need an excuse. I don't want to do it."

"Because you're afraid. You have this...magic."

"Magic!" She stared at him. Her? She was the quiet one. Her pies were special, she didn't deny that. But she had nothing to do with it. It was a gift, the way another woman was born with a beautiful singing voice. The way Gabe was born to captivate her. "This is too much."

Emotion rose up in her and she drew back from him. Her body started to shake on the inside, as if she were in the middle of an earthquake.

"Out." Her voice quaking, she pushed up from the chair. She was overreacting, she knew it, but right now she didn't care. "I just want you to leave. You didn't have to say that."

"You don't believe me." He shook his head, staying in his chair. "You really don't know how powerful you are."

"If I were powerful, you'd be a pile of ashes."

"Powerful doesn't mean the person who talks the loudest or laughs the loudest or has the most money." His gaze locked with hers, and she couldn't look away. "You're powerful because you care, and that shines out of you. You care about your dog, your friend, your grandmother. I know you cared for her. Love is powerful."

"You are..." She flailed her arms up. "Insane. Totally and horribly insane."

"Then humor an insane man." He smiled and once again his eyes glowed and she could practically feel him sending her waves of seduction that melted her muscles. "Do this for me. We'll try it a few times. It will prove who's right. You or me."

She plopped back down onto the chair. "I don't have to prove anything."

"Why does it scare you so much? You saw the bit." He gestured at the screen. "Once you relax, you're a natural. Even if I'm prejudiced because I want to sleep with you, there's no failure in this. No risk. People either watch you or they don't. If they do and we get ads, we'll make money. If they don't..." He shrugged. "The only one who will lose money will be me."

She sat stunned. She heard everything he said, but the only thing that stuck in her head was that he wanted to sleep with her. A squeaking sound came out of her mouth, but she couldn't form words. Her brain seemed to have turned into pureed pumpkin.

"I believe in you." His voice was even and calm. He kept staring straight into her eyes, compelling her to go along with him. "What I want to know is, do you believe in yourself?"

"Yes," she said fiercely. "Yes, I do."

He grinned and sat back. His intense gaze lessening, as if he were releasing her from a compulsion spell. Which was more crazy thinking. The result of reading the whole Harry Potter series. Real people didn't have compulsion spells. As for her magic pies... Some people could write songs by the time they were three. Others could do college math in third grade. She made pies.

Yes, they were magic, but everyone had magic. It's just that not everyone knew it.

"You know I meant..." She stopped, suddenly fighting laughter. "If Rosa gives her okay, I'll do it."

"Done." He slapped his hand on the table, as if he were sealing a deal. And he smiled at her like a man who'd just won the poker hand.

She guessed that made her the loser.

Slowly, she stood. This was the craziest day she could remember since she came to Miracle. This man was turning her calm and ordered life upside down.

"Do you have a card?" she asked. As if this were a normal conversation about business. As if he weren't crazier than her. Locked up, medicated and throw-away-the-key crazy. "I'll call you."

"Am I scaring you?" he asked. "Am I moving too fast?"

"Of course not."

"Then you won't mind if I do this." He stepped toward her, put his arm around her...and then he leaned so close to her she felt his breath on her skin. He pulled her against him and she closed her eyes and sighed, her body curving against his.

Acknowledgments

Special thanks to Amy Knupp and Natasha Fondren
for their editing skills. You are both amazing.

About Edie Ramer

Edie Ramer is funnier on the page than in real life. A
multiple award-winning writer, she writes stories with
heart, attitude, and magic. She lives in southeastern
Wisconsin with her husband, dog and one important cat.

Connect with Edie Online

www.edieramer.com
https://twitter.com/edieramer
http://www.facebook.com/edieramer.author

www.ingramcontent.com/pod-product-compliance
Lightning Source LLC
Chambersburg PA
CBHW022015170626
46808CB00001B/424